CODE OF THE BAR 10

Rancher Gene Adams takes three young wranglers with him to deliver forty steers to distant Fort Boone, leaving his most trusted confederates, Johnny Puma and Tomahawk, in charge of his vast Bar 10 ranch. But unknown to Gene, his arch enemy, the Wolf, has broken out of prison. Bent on vengeance, Wolf lies in wait, keen to torture Gene and his inexperienced cowboys. There seems to be no escape for the helpless rancher — unless, by a miracle, Johnny Puma and Tomahawk can save the situation . . .

MICHAEL D. GEORGE

◆

CODE OF THE BAR 10

Complete and Unabridged

LINFORD
Leicester

First published in Great Britain in 2001
under the name of 'Boyd Cassidy'

First Linford Edition
published 2003
by arrangement with
Robert Hale Limited
London

British Library CIP Data

George, Michael D.
    Code of the Bar 10.—Large print ed.—
Linford western library
    1. Western stories
    2. Large type books
    I. Title
    823.9′14 [F]

ISBN 0–7089–9963–8

Published by
F. A. Thorpe (Publishing)
Anstey, Leicestershire

Set by Words & Graphics Ltd.
Anstey, Leicestershire
Printed and bound in Great Britain by
T. J. International Ltd., Padstow, Cornwall

This book is printed on acid-free paper

Dedicated with thanks to the
memory of a wonderful lady,
Barbara Wilcox,
who was the 'Best in the West.'

Sleep peacefully.

Prologue

For many, vengeance will always be a place they have chosen not to ride into. A bitter trail with nothing but self-destruction at its end. Yet for one evil man known as the Wolf, vengeance was his only driving force. His only reason for returning from Hell.

To him, there was nothing else that mattered except seeking and administering revenge.

The Wolf had only been bested once in all his days, and the man who had achieved this dubious honour was the legendary rancher, Gene Lon Adams. Owner of the vast Bar 10 ranch. Adams and his men had managed to capture the notorious outlaw and see him sentenced to hard labour for life for his murderous crimes. That had been five long hot years ago. Time enough for the memory of the tall, broad-shouldered rancher to have faded.

Yet the Wolf had never forgotten the shame of being captured by a mere bunch of cowboys and sent shackled to the rat-infested penitentiary to the north of Texas.

There were those who had wanted to see the outlaw hanged but somehow he had managed to avoid this last indignity. Some said he had bribed the entire jury and perhaps even the judge, but what he had found in the prison had been far worse than any hangman's rope. For five years he had rotted in his own self-pity.

Five years of breaking rocks with a sledgehammer. Rocks which to the Wolf had been the skull of Gene Adams. A million times he had crushed that skull into dust.

Planning his ruthless revenge upon the rancher with the silver-white hair, the Wolf finally managed to make his escape. Having banked upon the greed of his henchmen, the Wolf had managed to spread rumours of a fortune he had hidden before his untimely capture. Rumours which eventually found the ears of his cohorts.

His gang were, like him, lacking anything remotely resembling honour, but when the news reached them of a fortune in gold stashed somewhere known only to the Wolf himself, they stormed the prison in force and freed their leader.

A small army had once again found their leader.

Five years had not mellowed the Wolf. They had only served to hone his hatred for Gene Adams.

Before his capture the Wolf had been a ruthless killer and robber with never a second thought for his victims, but now he was simply a creature bent only on revenge. Almost unrecognizable even to his closest men, only his acidic tones had remained the same. Only his voice told them who he was.

Still as cunning as his name implied, he had led his men two hundred miles to execute his plan. A plan which had festered and grown during his imprisonment.

His men did as they had always done and followed his orders blindly. The Wolf had always ensured they had plenty of money and this was another reason they had risked their lives in order to free him. Without the Wolf, they had been nothing more than second-rate outlaws crawling from one crime to the next, like the vermin they truly were.

Vengeance is mine, the Lord was often quoted as saying.

To the Wolf's way of thinking, he had more right to seek vengeance than any other living mortal. Even more right than God himself. He had been to a living hell which could not have been any worse than the one to which he knew his destiny would one day take him. The Wolf had always been an evil man but now he had no fear of anything death might offer.

Now he had become truly dangerous.

Whatever the cost, he would bring

Gene Adams into his well-laid trap and savour every second of his gradual destruction of the rancher.

The Wolf knew his men would do as he ordered or risk never being taken to his hidden stash of gold. Never share in the secreted wealth he taunted them with.

For Gene Adams, nothing would ever be the same again for either himself or any of his trusty riders of the Bar 10.

1

Fort Boone lay just three miles east of the border which separated Texas from Mexico. Fifteen miles away from the closest town and anything resembling civilization, it stood beaten by a thousand sandstorms for an entire generation. Once a stronghold boasting over two hundred cavalry troopers, it was now long past its days of glory. Now it was a mere relic boasting forty soldiers of dubious backgrounds waiting vainly for the Apache to return. Yet the Indians had long ceased to ride their painted ponies across these forgotten lands. Fort Boone stood for what had once been, but no longer was. A victim of its own success. Major Frank Bellamy had been there for nearly ten years and had witnessed the post's sad decline. This was his first command and, for all its faults, he had grown to respect this place. The army said this was where he belonged and Bellamy had never been the sort to argue with his betters. Duty was duty however boring it might have become. Tedium had rubbed shoulders for nearly a decade with complacency and Bellamy felt like a caged mountain-lion. He had once been a man of action and somewhere in the depths of his soul knew he still had at least one campaign left in him. One last chance to feel the thrill of the charge with an outheld sabre in his hand.

Once every week he sent out a patrol to ensure everything remained quiet along the border. It would keep them away from the fort for two nights and achieve nothing visible. A mere ten or twelve troopers led by a sergeant would ride in a circle of one hundred miles along the same route checking for anything unusual. For the ten years since he had been the commanding officer of Fort Boone, nothing had deviated from the norm. His men would return dusty and saddle-sore, with nothing to report. An ideal situation for most men but not for a man of Bellamy's insatiable spirit. Like a stray mustang who ventured too close to the perilous winding river beyond the border, he felt as if he were slowly sinking into a soft pitiless quicksand.

The fort was quite small by military standards but perfect for its situation. It could easily be defended by a hundred or so well-trained troopers, yet Bellamy now had less than a quarter of the original detachment at his disposal. Two large corrals lay outside the main walls where they kept their horses and also their beef-cattle. These were guarded by a solitary trooper. It had always seemed illogical to Bellamy for their livestock to be outside the protective walls of Fort Boone. Yet this was the way it had always been, and Bellamy knew it was foolhardy to even contemplate altering something which evidently worked. This was not the army way. If it ain't broke, don't fix it.

Major Frank Bellamy had no intention of fixing anything.

However mundane his life had become, his once boundless ambition continually thwarted by this place, Bellamy remained square-jawed and resolute.

Tuesday 12 April was crossed off the wall calendar with Bellamy's red pencil, which was then allowed to dangle on its string above the cracked shaving-mirror. The man moved to his office stove and gazed out of the small window at the parade ground as he sipped at his coffee thoughtfully. It was a good day. Bright and fresh. A true Texan day. For the first time for months he sensed a stirring in his soul which made his boots feel less heavy and uncomfortable. Today he would lead the small troop of soldiers on the weekly patrol himself. Today he felt as if something out there in the vast wilderness was calling to him. He had not even seen his horse for several months, but today he felt good. He grabbed at the door, pulled it wide open and shouted at the burly man standing less than ten feet from him.

'Sergeant Flynn? Get my horse saddled.'

The face of the faithful sergeant seemed to alter as he turned to confront the officer, who was pulling up his wide yellow suspenders over his broad shoulders.

'Did I hear you right, my old darlin'?' the Irish-flavoured accent enquired.

'You did, Sergeant Flynn,' Bellamy replied as he downed the last of his coffee.

'But it might rain. I'd hate for you to get a chill and be laid up for Easter.'

Bellamy lowered his head and glared at the man who had been with him for nearly twelve years.

'Cut the blarney, Flynn. Get my horse and do not call me darlin' ever again.'

'Right.' Flynn saluted.

'Right.' Bellamy nodded as he returned to the interior of his quarters.

The smiling sergeant touched his sun-bleached cavalry hat and obeyed. He moved like an old prize-fighter across the parade-ground towards the barracks where he would pass the order on to a lesser mortal. This was the army way and Flynn knew every single trick in the manual. A twenty-five-year cavalry man, he now faced his fiftieth summer with eyes that had seen more killing than he cared to recall. Fort Boone suited Flynn like a glove. Now as he felt the bones of his body telling him he was old, he wanted nothing more than to spend the final years of his career just drawing his pay. Bellamy wanted his mount saddled and readied and Flynn would ensure he got what he wanted. Flynn never shirked his duty and as he had only one main responsibility, keeping Bellamy happy, it never caused him to break out into a sweat. He had done it for so long, it had become a habit. If the commanding officer was content, everything within the fortress ran smoothly.

As the morning sun began to chase the long shadows off the parade-ground, it was as if the entire fort came to life at once to the eyes of the hardened army major. Tying his yellow bandanna around his wrinkled neck, Major Frank Bellamy could not help himself smiling proudly at the sight. Most of his men had been sent here as a punishment but he had managed to shape most of the bunch into something resembling soldiers. Pulling on his large white gauntlets, and stepping out into the morning sun, he wondered if they were a true fighting force. They had never been tested in battle and might never be required to do so, but it was still a question which troubled the officer as he headed for the mess-hall.

'Is my horse being readied, Flynn?' he asked as he passed the large Irishman.

'Yes indeedy, my old darlin'.'

'Make sure your mount is saddled too,' Bellamy ordered.

'My horse?' Flynn trailed the major

into the cool mess-hall, where the smell of breakfast greeted their nostrils.

'You, my friend, are coming with us.' Bellamy smiled.

For the first time for several years, Flynn found himself unable to find an answer worthy of his reputation. Being slapped heartily across his back did not help. Neither did the laughter which boomed from the lungs of the officer.

'You look ready for a hundred-mile ride around the countryside, Flynn,' Bellamy remarked loudly.

Sitting down next to his superior, the sergeant just nodded helplessly.

★　★　★

Bellamy sat astride his gleaming black charger feeling as if twenty years of his eventful life had melted beneath the burning heat of the sun. This was where he belonged, he thought. Atop a magnificent stallion, sabre in its scabbard hanging on his hip whilst he sat at the head of a troop of horsemen. There were only twelve men in this small line of cavalry but it felt like a hundred to the major. When Sergeant Flynn rode up to join him, Bellamy knew his company was complete. He cast his still-keen eyes over his men proudly, seeing not just soldiers but crusaders ready to right the world's ills.

Flynn rubbed his chin as he man-oeuvred his mount alongside the thoroughbred stallion.

'The men are ready, Major.'

'How many men are we leaving to protect the fort, Sergeant?'

Flynn did a quick calculation.

'About twenty-five or six.'

Bellamy nodded and spurred his horse forward towards the open gate-way slowly.

'Forward ho!'

The troop of soldiers steered their mounts after the major out into the arid landscape. For most of them it was a new experience, being led by the straight-backed officer. Yet there was no finer horseman in the cavalry, and within a few hundred yards of the fort they all knew it. He allowed his stallion almost to glide across the ground by simply holding his reins firmly in his gauntlet-covered hands. Turning the horse to the left, Bellamy somehow managed to get the creature up to speed without appearing to do anything. He had forgotten more about riding than any of his troopers had yet learned. With every stride of his horse's hoofs, his men seemed to gain in confidence behind him.

* * *

The small troop of cavalry had only been riding for a matter of twenty minutes; when the sand began to kick up and start cutting through them. The wind which swept down through the dry sun-baked gulch caused each man in turn to cover his mouth with his cavalry bandanna and tighten the drawstrings of his hat to prevent them being blown off. As they continued on, it was like riding into the stings of a million angry hornets. Yet even a million hornets would have been preferable to what lurked high above them, watching their every move.

Twenty well-armed riders had been studying the patrol from their vantage point since it had left the fort. Mounted in a long line across the ridge of the gulch, the men held their horses firmly in check as their leader sucked thoughtfully on a long black cigar.

These were no ordinary riders who studied the troop below them. These men were not here by accident. Their leader had brought them here for a single, deadly purpose.

He was called the Wolf and he wanted revenge.

2

Seated atop his chestnut mare Gene Lon Adams led the three riders towards the well-equipped hardware store. Johnny Puma sat on his pinto pony silently watching the citizens of Silver Springs moving about their daily chores as he kept pace. To their right, the bearded Tomahawk allowed his black quarter-horse to follow the others whilst he discreetly dozed, holding on to his reins. It was a skill he had taken a lifetime perfecting.

At Gene Adams's left, the fresh-faced Happy Summers rode his buckskin gelding silently. A chubby man, some-where in his thirties, Happy had been on the Bar 10 ranch for over a year doing odd jobs but had found that his true talents lay in wrangling. Adams was never slow at spotting a man's natural skills and soon gave Summers

18

the responsibility he deserved.

Coming into Silver Springs was a monthly ritual which seldom changed. Adams would buy everything his vast cattle ranch required whilst his top men would have a few cold beers. Back on the Bar 10 ranch another two dozen cowboys went about their chores expertly, knowing they were the envy of every rope-throwing Texan.

As the four horsemen drew to a halt before the store which was stocked with all sorts of vital provisions such as tin bath-tubs and leather goods, a voice called to them from across the wide street.

Adams turned in his saddle and rested his wrists upon the saddle horn as he stared at the small man moving towards them. It was Milt Greene, the telegraph-office operator.

'Hey, Gene. Got me a message for ya from a Major Bellamy at Fort Boone.'

Adams dismounted and walked to the centre of the street to greet the man.

'Thanks, Milt.'

Greene placed the wire into the gloved hands of the tall Texan and watched as he read it.

'A big order for the Bar 10, Gene.' Greene smiled.

Adams tossed him a silver quarter and grinned broadly.

'Ain't worth me arguing, considering you already read it, Milt. But it is a nice juicy order for the best beef in Texas.'

'Bar 10 beef,' Milt Greene added.

'Exactly.' Adams pushed the piece of paper into his coat pocket. 'When did this arrive?'

'Only about an hour back, Gene,' Greene replied.

'Send a return wire back for me, Milt. Tell him I'll cut out some prime stock and start for Fort Boone in the morning.'

Milt Greene held out his wrinkled hand.

'A dollar ought to cover it, Gene.'

Adams placed two silver dollars into

the soft-skinned palm of the old telegraph man and winked.

'Keep the change, Milt.'

'Always do, Gene. Always do,' Milt chuckled as he headed back towards his office.

Adams walked slowly back across the street and stepped up on to the sidewalk where his three companions waited.

'My old friend Major Frank Bellamy just wired me to bring forty steers to Fort Boone, boys.'

'Army a tad hungry, Gene?' Tomahawk yawned.

'Ten dollars a head hungry, old-timer,' Adams laughed.

Happy Summers sat on a flour barrel and began rolling a cigarette.

'I thought we drove about sixty longhorns over there two months back, Gene?'

Adams rubbed his chin thoughtfully.

'You could be right, Happy. When was that last herd of beef delivered to Fort Boone, Johnny?'

21

Johnny Puma chewed on his lower lip.

'Happy's right. It was the beginning of February and it's only just half-way through April now. They ain't due to order any more steers until the Fall, Gene.'

Adams shrugged, pulled out his long list and handed it to the youngster.

'Sixty head of longhorn on the hoof should have lasted them half a year, boys. Why would they order another forty steers now?'

Happy struck a match and inhaled the smoke from his cigarette.

'Maybe they had them rustled.'

'It's possible, I guess,' Adams mused.

'Makes the hairs on my neck tingle, Gene,' Johnny said.

Tomahawk yawned and looked around.

'When did we get here?'

Adams leaned down and tugged the old man's beard fondly.

'Tell me, Tomahawk. Exactly how many hours a working day do you sleep?'

Tomahawk rubbed his face with a sleeve and smacked his lips.

'I smells beer, boys.'

'You give this to old Pete in the store whilst me and the boys go and have a beer, Johnny,' Adams said, handing the provisions list to the youngest member of the small group.

Johnny walked into the store as the three other men stepped down into the bright sunshine and headed towards the saloon opposite.

Before the three cowboys had reached the bar, Johnny Puma had delivered the list of provisions and was walking right behind them.

'Four cold beers, Charlie,' Adams called out. He turned to look at the youthful grinning face of Johnny Puma. 'You're getting faster, boy. I reckon if you filed them spurs a tad, you might overtake us one of these days.'

Johnny rested his elbows upon the damp bar top and stared at the dozens of thimble glasses stacked before the long mirror. It was as if a hundred reflections bounced their images back at him.

'You still thinking about that wire, Johnny?' Adams asked as their beers were placed before them.

Johnny nodded.

'I guess so, Gene. It sure has me worrying.'

'How many steers did you take over to Fort Boone last time, Johnny? Are you sure it was sixty?'

'It was exactly sixty head,' Johnny answered as he recalled the drive. It was the first one he had led for the Bar 10.

All four men stood shoulder to shoulder, leaning on the bar for a few moments, sipping at their beers. Only Happy, who was puffing on his thin cigarette made any noise as he hummed a song whilst his pals pondered. It was true, the army only ever made two orders for beef-cattle during the year as a rule. Yet it was up to them how and when they spent their budget. Even so, Gene Adams was a man who did not like things which failed to add up in his straight-thinking brain.

'Do you want me to take this herd over to the fort as well, Gene?' asked Johnny Puma.

'I think I'll head this drive myself, Johnny.' Adams finished his beer and raised a finger to the bartender for refills.

'But, Gene?' Tomahawk piped up. 'I reckon young Johnny here can handle a simple forty head with a couple of wranglers. Besides, we have a lot of work on the ranch which needs you being there.'

Adams nodded. 'I know exactly how much work I have waiting for me back on the Bar 10, Tomahawk.'

'Me and Johnny could handle forty head, Gene,' Happy said through a haze of smoke as he sucked on the weed hanging from his lip.

'I don't doubt it, Happy. The thing is, I'm a mite curious about this wire, boys.' Adams watched as the beers were slid along the wet counter.

'It probably ain't nothing to fret

about, Gene.' Tomahawk lifted his glass and blew the froth from the rim.

'Maybe not.' Adams spotted his own reflection in the mirror and saw the expression etched upon his tanned face. Whatever his inner feelings, he was worried and it showed. As his gloved hand pulled the telegraph wire from his pocket his eyes focused upon the words carefully.

'What's wrong, Gene?' Tomahawk whispered.

'This wire asks me to bring the steers personally, old-timer.'

'That's odd.'

'Just a tad,' Adams agreed.

3

By nightfall Gene Adams's experienced men had cut out forty of their prime longhorn steers from the Bar 10's southern pastures and driven them up into the vast stock-pens beside the large ranch house and other buildings. The beef were well fattened on the long lush grasslands which made up most of the land, branded as the famous Bar 10. There were no better cattle anywhere in Texas and Adams knew it.

Adams stood on the porch of the house he had constructed with his own hands and watched as his men began drifting to their quarters in the various bunkhouses. Only Tomahawk, Johnny Puma and Happy Summers remained beside the tall rancher. He had said little since their return from Silver Springs and it was not like the man. He

27

had been troubled by the small scrap of paper in his pocket since learning of its contents. In all the years he had supplied beef to the army outpost, they had never insisted Adams himself should lead the drive.

'Four hundred dollars,' Tomahawk said as he removed his chaps and hung them over the porch railing next to the others.

'What did you say, old-timer?' Adams looked over his shoulder at the exhausted Tomahawk.

'Ain't that what them steers are worth, Gene?' Tomahawk toyed with his Indian axe as he moved to stand beside his boss.

'Yep. Four hundred,' Adams agreed. 'It's taken you ten hours to figure that out.'

'At least he got it right for once.' Johnny smiled as he removed his gunbelt and looped it over his shoulder.

Adams did not reply but continued staring out at the pens full of his moaning beef.

'This ain't like you, Gene.' Tomahawk rested a hand upon the man's shoulder.

Gene Adams gritted his teeth.

'I know, Tomahawk. I got me a feeling in my craw that just keeps chewing at me. Something just don't feel right about this deal.'

'Sometimes it pays to listen to your instincts and not your head, Gene.' The old man watched as Happy and Johnny walked into the illuminated house.

'I ain't gonna turn my back on four hundred bucks,' Adams sighed.

'That's the spirit.' Tomahawk slapped the back of his long-time friend.

'Hell. I'm starting to act like an old woman, Tomahawk.' Adams laughed as he turned and led his bearded friend into the warmth of the house. 'Maybe it's because we've had such a darn quiet winter I'm seeing things that ain't really there.'

'Sure enough. I guess you and me is just a mite long in the tooth for anything exciting, Gene.' Tomahawk scratched his beard.

'We ain't that old, Tomahawk,' Adams laughed.

'Well I ain't, but you've had snow under your 'John B' for an awful long time.' Tomahawk nodded to himself.

'At least my stove is still lit, you darn rascal.'

Tomahawk nodded again as they closed the door behind them and inhaled the aroma of cooking T-bone steaks emanating from the kitchen. Tomahawk too had the same feeling gnawing at his insides. Sometimes trouble could be spotted a mile off as it rode towards you. Sometimes danger was only a brief fragrance on the breeze. Whatever these men were feeling could not be seen or avoided, only dreaded like a deadly invisible enemy.

★   ★   ★

A solitary rooster signalled the coming of daybreak on the Bar 10 ranch. Gene

Adams was already dressed and waiting at the stock-pens when his men began drifting out from their bunkhouses for the new day. Adams said nothing as he leaned on the top fence-pole, watching the animals milling around before him. His mind drifted back to how it had all started four decades earlier, when he had arrived at this place with a mere dozen head of longhorn cattle and a big dream. Now there were ten thousand head of his carefully bred stock roaming his massive ranch, each bearing his unique brand. His cattle were the envy of all who encountered them. Fat and sassy like the land itself.

The Bar 10 had never ceased to amaze him. Knee-high sweet grassland from one horizon to the next had made his dream a reality and he was grateful. Wealth beyond calculation had been given to Gene Lon Adams but it had cost him more than he could or would admit. Adams had sacrificed many things in his pursuit of making this ranch what it now was. Every cent he possessed had been earned and he had the scars to prove it. Over the years Adams had broken probably half the bones in his body fighting for this ranch and yet he still loved it. It had been moulded by his own hands and his own unwavering faith. Yet after more than forty years trouble was still a regular visitor to the Bar 10. Even now he could not relax like other men, because there was always someone out there waiting to try and take it away from him the moment he dropped his guard.

Texas was no place for the weak of heart or spirit. It was a place where only real men survived and prospered. Adams was one of that rare breed of men.

He removed his black ten-gallon hat, beat the dust off it against his chaps and watched as his rannies went about their duties confidently, knowing he had to do something that would upset his two most loyal companions. He had slept little during the night thinking about the strange telegram. The only conclusion he had arrived at was that this seemingly routine cattle-drive was fraught with potential danger. A danger Adams did not wish to inflict upon either Tomahawk or the young hot-headed Johnny.

If he was wrong, nothing would be lost by leaving his two best friends on the ranch. If he were correct, at least they would be safe and not forced into fighting his battles for him yet again. Adams had made many enemies over the years. Success, he knew, bred contempt and envy in even the most solid of citizens but sometimes there was a greater force which drove danger to his doorstep. Adams felt Johnny and Tomahawk deserved to be spared yet another battle. The trouble was, how was he going to break it to them?

Then Gene Adams's keen eyes saw Johnny Puma heading towards him dressed for the trail. Adams had made a decision which he knew would not sit easily on the young cowboy's excitable shoulders. Yet he knew it was the right decision.

'We ready to head out, Gene?' Johnny asked as he reached the corral.

'You ain't coming with me, Johnny,' Adams said in a low voice as he stared at the ground between them.

Johnny stood as if frozen to the spot, stunned by the statement.

'Let me hear that again, Gene?'

Adams glanced across at his young friend.

'You're staying here, Johnny.'

The youngster felt as if he had been kicked hard in his guts as the words hit him. For a moment he was unable to say anything. He edged closer to the man he had grown to think of as a father.

'But, Gene. Wherever you go, I go.'

'Not this time.' Adams found it tough to look at Johnny as he spoke.

Neither man continued with their talking as Tomahawk and Happy approached from the stables.

'We ready to go, boys?' Tomahawk piped up.

'You ain't going, old-timer,' Adams said bluntly.

Tomahawk pushed his battered Stetson back off his face and gazed in bewilderment at his friend.

'Quit ya joshing, Gene. What ya mean I ain't going?'

'Gene ain't taking me either, Tomahawk,' Johnny informed the old man.

Tomahawk moved closer to the rancher.

'Hey, Gene. Stop this tomfoolery, son.'

Adams narrowed his eyes. 'You and Johnny are staying here to look after the Bar 10 for me, old-timer.'

'This don't figure, Gene,' Tomahawk growled.

'It don't figure at all,' Johnny concurred.

'It does to me, boys,' Adams snapped as he placed his hat back over his white hair and moved away from the fence-poles.

The three cowboys trailed the rancher down through an avenue of trees, along a narrow path between the two enormous corrals and, emerging into the bright sunshine, up towards the small pond which helped keep the area so green.

'I'm taking Happy and two of the other boys on this drive.'

Happy Summers felt uneasy as Adams raised a gloved hand and pointed straight at him.

'Any preference, Gene?'

'Get Tom and Larry, Happy. Tell them to pack some grub and water on to the old prairie schooner. We'll be away a week or more.' Adams sucked in the cool air off the water as he spoke.

Tomahawk watched silently as Happy headed back towards the bunkhouses. Then he moved in front of Adams.

'Something ain't sitting right, Gene. Something ain't sitting right, at all.'

'Me and Tomahawk always tag along, Gene,' Johnny added.

Gene Adams raised himself up to his

full height and faced his men squarely.

'I don't need you on this trip, boys.'

'But we is a team,' Tomahawk protested.

'Tom and Larry are better wranglers than either of you varmints. I need good wranglers on this drive, not a young rooster and an old man who sleeps half the day.'

The two men were stunned by the aggression of Gene Adams's words as he broke away from them and strode off. Neither had ever felt so utterly useless before.

4

Larry Baker sat uneasily across the driver's seat of the wagon toying with the reins to the four-horse team. From his vantage-point he could see more than any of the other Bar 10 cowhands, and what he saw, made him wary. For the first time in the three or so years Larry had worked on the vast Texan cattle ranch, he had seen Gene Adams turn mean. Not with him or any of the other wranglers, but with his two best friends, Tomahawk and Johnny Puma. Whatever the reason for this complete change of character, the slow-witted Larry Baker could only guess. Not being a man of great imagination, he simply sat totally bemused. He and fellow wranglers Happy Summers and Tom Conners had stocked the broad-beamed converted prairie schooner with supplies just as Adams had ordered. The chuck-box was full to overflowing with provisions ranging from pinto beans to dried fruit and flour, enough to last them a month if necessary. The water-barrel strapped to the side of the wagon was full with fresh-drawn crystal clear liquid from the deep well. Yet Happy, Tom and the watching Larry knew that only they and the brooding Adams would taste that water on this drive.

Every single ranch hand seemed incapable of even looking at either Adams or the confused Tomahawk and the stunned, fretting Johnny. What had occurred to create such a sad sight? Larry sat watching the scene below him like a man waiting for a lightning strike, the air was so full of electricity.

Since Adams had made his decision not to take Tomahawk or Johnny, it seemed as if every cowboy on the Bar 10 was walking on eggshells. None of the dozens of men dared open his mouth for fear of bringing the wrath of the rancher down upon himself. If

Adams could turn on his best pals so unexpectedly, what might he do to the simple rannies?

Not one of the experienced cattle-men had ever known the atmosphere to be so tense. Usually the Bar 10 ran like a well-greased machine, everyone knowing just how far they could push Adams. Yet, as the men readied the herd for the drive, it was unusually quiet. Only the sound of the irate longhorns echoed around the Bar 10 this day. It was as if every man had been struck mute. Gene Adams had checked his chestnut mare at least ten times while he waited for the prepara-tions to be completed. Larry Baker had silently observed the rancher getting on and off his horse every few minutes during the previous hour. First he'd checked his cinch, then each of the horse's legs in turn. Then he'd seemed to repeat his actions, unaware that he was being watched. Larry knew that whatever the big man might have said, he was not himself without his two friends around him.

It just failed to make any sense.

After helping to load the chuck-wagon, Tom Conners had saddled his small grey cutting-horse and was moving around within the corral wearing his red bandanna backwards over his mouth and nose, as he cut out the longhorns one by one before chasing them into the funnelling-chute. A cloud of dust seemed to hang over the corral as the beasts tore up the dry sun-baked ground. When Tom had a dozen head lined up along the chute, Happy opened the gate and waved a saddle rope until the steers began following Gene Adams, astride his tall chestnut mare, out into the main pasture. Tom remained within the dust-choked confines of the corral until he had sent all of the large aggressive steers out after the others. Only then did he signal to Larry to start the chuck-wagon rolling as he rode down the chute and into position. Within a few hundred yards of the heart of the ranch, the herd took shape: Adams at the point, Happy on the left flank and Tom directly opposite on the right. Trailing the herd at the drag, Larry drove the chuck-wagon, cracking his bullwhip every few yards to keep the creatures moving at pace.

A mere forty head was almost a dream job for the skilled cowboys. They had driven thousands of steers up to the railhead at McCoy in their time. As Gene Adams led the small herd he could not see the faces of the three men behind him as they communicated using hand signals to one another above the dust kicked up by the agitated cattle. These three wranglers were indeed the best on the Bar 10 but they had never been first choice to accompany Adams before. All three wondered why they had been picked out this time. Each of them felt as if he had upset his friends, Tomahawk and Johnny, by replacing them. Happy Summers turned in his saddle and waved farewell to the two pathetic figures standing beside the corral. The wave was not returned.

As the herd disappeared out of sight, the two dejected cowboys moved aimlessly about the scene until Johnny pulled the heavy corral-gate shut. He stood leaning on the top pole and a hand came to rest on his shoulder. Johnny Puma and Tomahawk stood alone as the other rannies went about their chores trying hard to avoid them.

'I still don't get it, Tomahawk,' the young man said as he kicked at the dirt.

'Nope. It don't make a lotta sense, boy.' Tomahawk swallowed hard. 'I ain't never heard Gene talk like that to nobody, especially us. He was acting like a critter who just swallowed loco beans.'

The two friends turned and wandered under the shade of some tall broadleafed trees.

'He practically called us useless,' Johnny moaned.

'Yep. He was kinda gritty with his tongue all right,' Tomahawk agreed,

They found the long bench that overlooked the pond and sat down together.

'Am I a hothead?' Johnny pulled off his Stetson and rested it on his knee.

'Do I fall asleep during the day?' queried Tomahawk.

Both men shrugged.

'How come he left us here?' Johnny asked.

Tomahawk plucked a long grass stem from beside the bench and began sucking on it thoughtfully.

'It don't figure, boy.'

Johnny stared out at the gleaming water before them and sighed heavily.

'Tom and Larry are pretty good wranglers, I guess.'

'Happy is darn good too,' Tomahawk admitted.

There was a long silence between the two men as they tried to understand how Gene Adams could have turned on them so unexpectedly. After a few moments a loud noise reverberated from the nostrils of the older man who then jumped up as if startled by the sound.

'You hear that, Johnny? Did the hogs get loose?'

Johnny shook his head rose to his feet and slapped his hat across Tomahawk's britches.

'Yep, I heard it OK. You was snoring again, you old sidewinder.'

Tomahawk felt an ache in the pit of his stomach.

'Maybe I am getting a tad long in the tooth, Johnny.'

'You ain't got no damn teeth, old-timer,' the youngster laughed.

5

The small herd of longhorn cattle had covered close to fifteen miles by the end of the first day, every mile lush in grass never less than knee high. Adams had made camp and decided they would each ride night guard for three hours whilst the others slept. Happy Summers had drawn short straw and was out circling the steers first. The jovial man actually preferred being in his saddle rather than sitting face to face with Adams. Adams still was not his usual self and the air around the camp had an unpleasant feel to it.

The sun seemed to hang in the Texas sky for an eternity after the small group had eaten, but as it eventually dipped below the horizon, the tension began to subside. As the sky ran red with the day's farewell, Gene Adams walked alone around the small encampment's boundaries before reaching the chuck-wagon. Adams leaned over the tailgate of the chuck-box and soaked in the last of the crimson rays as a million stars began to appear above them.

He had seen many sunsets during his time but none as haunting as this one. Gazing across the flat land beyond the wagon he could hear Happy singing as he circled the resting cattle. Their long horns began to catch the light of the new moon as they protruded above the lush tall grass. It was an eerie sight.

A cold chill ran over Adams's entire body as he stared down at Tom and Larry curled up in their bedrolls beside the roaring camp-fire. They had been asleep not long after wrapping themselves in their thick rough blankets, yet Adams could not sleep. His mind kept thinking about Major Bellamy at Fort Boone. A man he had known for a decade.

Adams knew that Major Bellamy had no actual reason for wanting to meet him face to face. If there was something important to discuss, he would have said so in the telegram. Bellamy was not the sort to waste anyone's time. The rancher pulled the scrap of paper from his pocket for the umpteenth time and leaned under the oil lamp hanging on the chuck-box to study it again. He had been too long in Texas not to know when something just didn't add up. Men like Adams had a sixth sense about such things. Folks lacking that sixth sense were buried out there under the sacred Texas soil. This was a land that did not allow anyone a second chance.

This simple wire just did not add up. He lowered the wick on the lantern and turned to gaze down at the roaring fire once more. Maybe he was wrong in bringing these rannies along instead of his two trusty friends. If trouble was waiting for them out there at Fort Boone, maybe he just might require the skilled guns of Johnny and the deadly accuracy with the Indian hatchet of old Tomahawk.

As he finished the last of the coffee he felt a mixture of emotions welling up inside him. He felt happy that he had left his two best friends behind at the ranch where they would be safe but angry at the way he had bad-mouthed them. His choice of words had been totally wrong. Yet he knew sometimes it paid to be cruel if you intended to protect those you cared for. However much he reasoned with himself, he could not get the bitter taste from his mouth.

He had hurt them. In doing so, he had hurt himself.

As Adams strolled to the line of tethered horses he wondered if his instincts were correct. Was he riding into something far more dangerous than he could possibly imagine? Or was he just allowing his own nightmares to invade the normality of a simple telegraph message?

If trouble was waiting for them, could Tom, Larry and Happy manage to defend themselves? Was he taking three innocent cowboys to their deaths?

Should he warn them of his own fears? These men were not like Johnny Puma, who had been an outlaw before finding sanctuary with him on the Bar 10. They did not have the background of Tomahawk who had lived with Indians decades before setting eyes upon his first white face. Both had grown up fighting for survival before becoming cowboys. They, like Adams himself, had a fire in their bellies which still burned.

Tom, Happy and Larry were just plain simple wranglers. No more and no less. Adams doubted whether they had ever used their guns for anything except seeing off the odd coyote or cougar. Could they fight for their lives if necessary?

Adams moved to the camp-fire and sat down on his bedroll. Staring into the flames of the fire he felt its warmth against his face. As he lay down, he knew sleep would not visit him this night.

This night he would stare at the flames and be unable to get all the thoughts out of his mind. This night would be real long.

★　★　★

It might have been the moon which cast its blue glowing light across the ranch house set at the heart of the Bar 10, as well as over the far-off herd of longhorns, but to the pair of cowboys standing upon the porch it was merely another taunting reminder; they were not camping beneath the canopy of stars this night.

The older of the two men ran a double-edged blade along a whetstone as he rested a hip on the wooden railing. The blade was keen and glistened in the light of the oil lantern, but the old hands continued to polish its deadly sharpness anyway.

The younger man brooded silently, resting the palms of his hands upon the grips of his matched Colts, and stared thoughtfully up at the sky.

Tomahawk finally broke up the silence as he rested the stone upon the top of the railings and slid the axe into his broad belt over his left hip.

'How far do you reckon they've gotten, Johnny?'

The youngster turned his head and looked at his friend.

'Between ten and twenty miles?'

'Sounds about right.' Tomahawk walked to the side of his pal and rested his butt upon the wooden railings as their eyes met.

'What you thinking, old-timer?' Johnny asked.

'Same as you, I guess.'

'I'm thinking about saddling up and riding out after Gene and the boys, Tomahawk,' Johnny Puma admitted.

Tomahawk nodded. 'Like I said, same as you.'

Johnny sighed heavily as he edged closer to the older cowboy.

'You was thinking about heading out after Gene?'

'Sure thing.' Tomahawk ran his hand over his whiskers. 'I done me a mess of thinking since supper. Gene chewed us out for no reason and that means only one thing.'

'What?'

'He was scared to take us along in case we got ourselves shot up, Johnny.' The old man screwed up his wrinkled eyes and glared at his junior. 'Gene had a bad feeling about that telegram from Fort Boone. It just didn't sit right on his craw. He was trying to save our necks, in case he was right.'

Johnny Puma leaned next to the old man.

'Them steers could have made only about thirteen miles before sundown, old-timer. How long do you reckon it would take to catch up with them?'

'Reckon if we started at first light, we might catch up with them before they reach Fort Boone.' Tomahawk's sharp eyes began to brighten as he spoke.

'What if we headed out now?' the young man suggested.

Tomahawk stood and shook his head.

'I ain't hankering to ride in the dark, boy.'

Johnny turned his partner and pointed up at the brilliant full moon.

'It ain't that dark, Tomahawk. If'n we started now, we could catch Gene and the boys before nightfall tomorrow.'

The older man shrugged.

'Saddle our horses and fill a few extra canteens, boy. We is going for a ride.'

6

With moonlight as their only ally, the two riders left the peaceful safety of the Bar 10 just before midnight and headed west. Neither had ever ridden this route after nightfall before and although the crisp blue moon highlighted the terrain, it gave no clue as to what lay beneath the blanket of tall grass. Even a mere forty head of well-fattened longhorn steers left their mark on the ground beneath the tall swaying grass. Neither rider wished risking their mounts snapping a leg in the hidden furrows, yet they rode on, gaining pace with every passing minute.

Standing in his stirrups, Tomahawk followed Johnny's pinto pony on his black quarter-horse. Both riders had no belly for the speed they were forcing their mounts to find, but there was no time to ponder the risks. They had to make up ground as quickly as possible and they both knew it.

Johnny began to realize that forcing their horses relentlessly on in pursuit of the distinctive trail left by the herd would take them too long. Dragging his reins hard to the right, the young man turned to head for the vast range of rolling hills to the north. This course could take hours off their journey. With the old-timer glued to Johnny Puma's pinto's tail, they soon began to make progress.

Galloping over the steep hills and along the perilous ridges was the only chance they had of reducing the distance between themselves and the herd of longhorns led by Adams. Johnny knew Adams had to stick to the valley trails which wove between the heart of the vast Bar 10 and the distant fortress. Steers were dumb but not dumb enough to be led over hills when a sweet grassy valley presented itself.

The pair of cowboys drove their horses hard into the night across the crests of dangerous tree-topped mountain trails and along seldom-used tracks. The bright moon was high overhead as Tomahawk spurred his black mount after the climbing pinto into the heart of the high country. This was no ride for the faint-hearted, but these men were never afraid to take risks when it came to helping Gene Adams. For him, they would wrestle with a sack of sidewinders.

As they raced across a narrow mountain ledge both men knew they had managed to save themselves at least two miles on the route used by Gene and his trail drivers. They drew their mounts to a stop and quickly watered the animals while they tried to work out the best route down to the distant plains. It was a strange spot beneath the bright moon where Tomahawk and Johnny found themselves resting. There was a cutting cold edge to the breeze which whipped over the two men and their exhausted mounts.

'If we take the high trail, I figure we

can catch Gene before noon tomorrow,'
Johnny said, taking a mouthful of water
before handing the canteen to his pal.

Tomahawk swilled water around his
dry mouth before spitting at the
ground.

'You ever ridden that trail, Johnny?'

'Once or twice. Why?'

'Why? 'cos it's darn dangerous, that's
why. This whole damn mountain has a
habit of sliding away after a big rain.'
The old man retrieved his hat from
between his horse's legs and placed it
on his head. 'We had us a real big rain
last month.'

'It's our best bet though.' Johnny
pulled his gloves tightly over his hands
and gathered up his loose reins.

'Taking the lower trail is a lot safer,
boy.'

'Safer, but twice as long, Tomahawk.'

'We could still catch up with the herd
before it reaches Fort Boone, Johnny.'
Tomahawk's words hung in the thin
air.

Johnny nodded as he stepped into his

stirrup and slowly pulled himself up on to the pinto.

'I'm taking the high trail. Are ya with me, oldtimer?'

Tomahawk mounted his quarterhorse and gently spurred it alongside the pony.

'OK. Reckon I'll tag along just in case you needs me.'

The two riders aimed their horses through the tall trees and up into the high country. The trail here was narrower than any they had encountered during their journey and rose at an alarming rate. Tomahawk gripped his saddle horn as he followed the younger man's lead. Every step his horse took as it climbed up the slippery incline made the old man's heart beat faster and faster. Yet he followed.

Reaching a level trail the two riders began spurring their horses again until the mountain once more faced them like a terrifying wall. Undaunted by the trail as it started to wind its way up the twisting route once more, Johnny Puma led the way whilst Tomahawk followed. Now steeper and less forgiving, the trail grew softer as it skimmed the very edge of a damp treacherous cliff. Trees somehow managed to remain rooted to their precarious perches, and the riders passed carefully by them on their steady ascent. Then the trail dipped down through a black mass of bushes and low hanging branches where even the bright moonlight seemed unable to penetrate. Johnny led the way by spurring his unwilling pony on through the dense undergrowth with Tomahawk close behind. The ground was unstable and damp beneath the hoofs of their unwilling mounts. Suddenly, Johnny felt his horse sliding closer and closer towards the cliff edge. Using every ounce of his strength the youthful rider fought with his reins as he tried to stop his pony from slipping off the mountain, and falling into the black void below.

Somehow the pinto found a grip and steadied itself. Pulling his pinto up short, Johnny hovered above a horrifying drop as Tomahawk drew level with him.

'I thought we was goners then, boy,' Tomahawk gulped as he gripped a tree branch in one hand and his reins in the other.

'You and me both,' Johnny admitted.

Staring down, neither man could see anything amid the dense shadows of the trees. Johnny turned carefully, looked back at the greasy clay slope down which they had slid to find themselves here, a mere few feet from the deadly precipice. For a moment he felt sick as he began to realize that the old man had been correct about this mountain's habit of allowing its trails to simply fall away into oblivion.

'If this was the old high trail, it sure ain't any longer,' Tomahawk said, holding his reins tightly in his gloved hands.

Johnny Puma rubbed the sweat from his face and tried to focus on the black mystery below them. Even the moonlight belied their exact location amid the swirling mist.

'I thought the trail cut off down to the left, Tomahawk.'

Tomahawk moved his horse closer to the edge of the treacherous chasm, still clinging to the tree branch in case the ground disappeared from beneath them.

'In this half light, it looks to me like our trail got itself washed away, boy.'

Johnny swallowed deeply. 'I ain't been up here in over a year. Could an entire side of the mountain just get washed away, old-timer?'

'I guess so.' Tomahawk stood in his stirrups and cautiously leaned out to try and see what was below the edge of the ridge.

'See anything?'

'Nope. Just a lotta black.'

Johnny dismounted and handed his reins to Tomahawk as he moved slowly to the very edge of the drop. The ground was brittle and suddenly fell away under his high-heeled Cuban boots, causing him to grab out desperately for his stirrup. Feeling his legs slipping into space, the young cowboy held on to the saddle as he fell. For a terrifying moment, Johnny felt his entire body hanging in mid-air. Staring up at his pinto, he began to pray his cinch strap would hold.

'Johnny?' Tomahawk yelled as he saw his pal disappearing from view.

'Stay in your saddle, old man,' Johnny called up as he held firmly on to the stirrup whilst his legs searched for something to stand on. For nearly an entire minute the youngster swayed in mid-air, trying to find a foothold. There was nothing.

Tomahawk wrapped his partner's reins around his own saddle horn and pulled up at his own reins, urging his quarter-horse to walk backwards away from the edge of the sheer drop on to firmer, drier ground. Slowly, the mount began to obey and shy away from the crumbling cliff. Just as slowly the pinto pony began to step back and haul its master away from the deadly drop.

When Johnny Puma felt his legs being dragged back on to the rough ground he staggered upright and leaned over his saddle silently.

'You OK, Johnny?' Tomahawk shouted as he saw the Stetson buried into the pinto's saddle.

'Yep,' the young cowboy gasped, looking over his pony at his distraught friend. 'I thought I was a goner there for a while, Tomahawk.'

'You and me both.' Tomahawk slid off his saddle and tied his reins to a tree-trunk before moving carefully to his pal.

'We better wait until sun-up before carrying on.' Johnny Puma sighed heavily as he felt every muscle in his torso screaming out in agony beneath his shirt.

'Reckon we ought to get some shut-eye. We ain't going anywhere tonight, boy,' Tomahawk snorted.

7

The first rays of the morning sun raced across the mountains and awoke the pair of Bar 10 riders by its brilliance. Tomahawk seemed to be up on his feet far faster than his young companion. What he saw made his blood freeze. Kicking at the boots of Johnny Puma until he opened his eyes, Tomahawk stood open-mouthed, staring in awe at the scene before him.

'What's so darn urgent, old man?' Johnny asked as he stretched his bones free of their stiffness.

'Open ya eyes, sonny,' Tomahawk gulped as his friend staggered to his side.

Rubbing his eyes, Johnny began to understand the urgency.

'Oh my Lord.'

Tomahawk nodded. 'Reckon we was luckier than we figured last night.'

The two men stood looking at the scene bathed in the light of explanation before them. Now as the sun soaked everything in its brilliant illumination, the two souls could finally see how close they had come to falling a half-mile down into a tree-covered canyon. The sight did not make them feel any the better, rather it chilled their bones in its stark terrifying reality.

Cautiously stepping towards the deadly chasm, Johnny shied away from making the same mistake he had made the previous night. The ground was red with moist wet clay. The young man gazed at the tracks of his desperate slide upon the pony and then he felt the hairs on the nape of his neck tingle as he could see where he had almost fallen to his death.

'Its a long way down, Tomahawk.'

The older man agreed.

'Yep. A darn long way down, boy.'

Johnny tried to visualize where the old trail had once been and then felt a shiver in his spine.

'I figure about twenty feet of this darn mountain must have just fallen away since I was last up here, Tomahawk.'

'I told you.' Tomahawk gazed around them as he moved cautiously to where he had firmly secured their horses. There was no trail ahead of them and he knew it. Running his weathered hand over the neck of his black mount, Tomahawk wondered if they had been wise to even attempt catching up with Gene Adams. The rancher was not a man to be disobeyed lightly. Yet, the more he thought about it, he knew they were right to try. Even if Adams chewed them out, at least they would be on hand if something were to occur.

Johnny stepped back to the firmer ground closer to his pal.

'OK. You were right and I was wrong. Do you reckon we can still catch up with Gene?'

'Sure we can, boy,' Tomahawk replied.

'Good job we stopped when we

stopped.' Johnny swallowed deeply as he pointed to the unstable cliff edge.

'Now we've gotta backtrack down to where we watered the horses last night and take the trail I favoured.' The older man sniffed, rubbing his beard.

Johnny nodded. 'I'm angry with my own stupidity.'

'Ain't your fault, boy.' Tomahawk rested a hand on his friend's arm. 'If this trail had still been here, we would have made real good time.'

'But now we've lost at least half a day.' Johnny shook his head as he stared over his shoulder at the incredible view. A view which reached out towards the plains where he knew the small herd was headed.

'We can still catch up with Gene and the boys before they gets to Fort Boone,' Tomahawk comforted. 'I know a safe route which will take us over Sugar Loaf Mesa. A tough ride, but safe.'

Carefully the two men untied their horses and led them up through the bushes on to firmer, more solid ground, where they felt safer in mounting the rested creatures. It was a long ride down the precarious route which they had climbed during the moonlit hours. Now it seemed even more perilous as the sunlight revealed all the dangers which had been hidden previously.

★ ★ ★

Painted Rock was just another small Texas town on the edge of civilization. Lying fifty miles east of the remote Fort Boone in the middle of an area renowned for sand-storms and flies, it somehow managed to remain valuable to the passing travellers who used its various facilities. Its telegraph office was the end of the line and in itself a precious addition to the town. The wires on their bleached poles did not go any further west than Painted Rock. Mexico lay just a few miles past the fortress and the telegraph company knew there was no profit to be made in the land of the siesta.

Major Frank Bellamy steered his mount down the centre of the drab main street, followed by his ragged troop of cavalry. As he was leading this patrol, he had decided to make it the most thorough of the year.

Sergeant Flynn spurred his flagging mount until he drew level with his commanding officer as they approached the livery stables situated next to a busy saloon.

'Can we have ourselves a little dram, me old darling?'

Bellamy cringed.

'Water?'

Flynn screwed up his face in horror.

'Water is for washing. Whiskey is for drinking.'

The major dismounted and watched as his men began to follow suit behind him. Flynn somehow managed to get himself in front of the exhausted officer.

'Can I tell the men they can go into the saloon and toast your health, sir?'

Bellamy rolled his eyes and nodded.

'I imagine so. You can come with me, Flynn.'

Sergeant Flynn's jaw dropped to his chest.

'But . . . '

Bellamy turned to look down the sun-soaked, windswept street and caught sight of the familiar features of the telegraph operator waving at him from his office.

'What does old Wally want, Flynn?'

Flynn followed the major across the street.

'I have no idea what the little man wants, me old darling.'

As the two soldiers stepped up on to the side-walk the telegraph office door opened and the small-framed man stepped out to greet them with a concerned expression etched into his features.

'Major Bellamy. I reckon you ought to look at this wire I was ordered to send a couple of days past.'

Bellamy accepted the scrap of paper and read it.

'Who ordered you to send a wire in my name to Gene Adams?'

'A real ugly man. There were a dozen or more of them and I did as I was told because the ugly critter held a gun at my head.'

Bellamy patted Wally on the shoulder and turned away thoughtfully.

'What's wrong, me darling?' Flynn asked.

'Tell the men to get a meal and a few drinks,' Bellamy said grimly.

'That's more like it,' Flynn gushed.

Staring at his pocket-watch, the officer made a mental calculation.

'Get the horses rubbed down, watered and fed. We ride back for the fort in exactly three hours.'

★ ★ ★

On the tail end of the third day, just as the sun was beginning to set, Gene Adams brought the small herd of prime Bar 10 steers up over a small mesa and at last caught sight of their objective.

Fort Boone stood eerily silent upon its sandy foundations as the broad-shouldered rancher pulled in his reins. It was nearly dark as he stood in his stirrups and pondered the sight before them. The fort was a good two miles away and yet even as darkness overwhelmed the distance between them, Adams knew something was not right.

Death seemed to be out there in the heart of what should have been their sanctuary. The air had the aroma of something which was making his chestnut mare nervous.

Happy Summers rode up beside the rancher as Tom Conners forced the longhorns to a halt a few hundred yards behind them. Dragging his reins up to his chest, Summers screwed up his eyes and stared out at the strangely silent fortress.

'How come there ain't no lights showing from the fort, Gene?'

'That's been bothering me too, Happy,' Adams admitted as he wrestled with his anxious mount.

'Them soldier-boys usually hang a few lanterns around the place at sundown, as I recall.' Happy ran his hand along the lathered neck of his buck-skin.

Adams gritted his teeth.

'They usually have a flag flying on that pole. Can you see any sign of 'Old Glory'?'

'Nope, Gene. I reckon there ain't no flag flying on that there pole.' Happy felt his mouth growing dryer. 'Maybe they take it down after sunset.'

'Maybe,' Adams grunted. He sniffed the air. 'Can you smell that, Happy?'

Happy raised his head and inhaled.

'What is that, Gene?'

'I reckon something's dead out there, son,' Adams replied. He gripped his reins tightly.

'Whatever it is, it's spooking the horses,' Happy noted.

'What you looking at?'

'Are them buzzards circling over yonder?' Happy pointed at a few birds swooping off into the darkness.

Adams pulled in his reins tighter as he forced his mount to turn away from the scene and head back down towards the waiting herd. Happy trailed the rancher until they arrived beside the chuck-wagon where Tom was drinking from the water barrel while holding on to his reins.

Adams dismounted, moved to the wagon and leaned against the rear wheel. It was as if every nerve in his body was screaming out as he tried to calm himself.

'What's wrong, Gene?' Larry asked when he climbed down from the chuck-wagon. He moved towards the small trio of men.

'Trouble, if I ain't mistaken, Larry. Big trouble,' Adams drawled.

'How come we don't take the herd in?' Happy asked. He pulled out the makings for a cigarette from his shirt-pocket and began rolling himself a smoke.

The eyes of the rancher narrowed.

'Remember the smell, Happy?'

Happy struck a match along his saddle horn and drew the flame to his cigarette before exhaling the smoke.

'We might be wrong.'

'I've been to this fort more times than I can remember, boys. I ain't never seen the place in darkness after sundown.'

Larry rubbed his sore neck.

'How many soldier-boys should there be, Gene?'

'A few dozen at least,' Adams replied as he stepped past his men and stared out at the blackness before them. 'Enough men to make a little noise. Listen.'

'I don't hear nothing,' Happy said. His tongue rolled his cigarette around his jaw.

'Exactly, Happy. It's like the grave out there.' Adams flicked the safety loops off his gold-plated pistols. 'If them soldiers are dead, like I reckon, we better be darn careful we don't end up joining them.'

Larry moved close to the rancher.

'What we gonna do?'

'We can't take the risk of making camp,' Adams sighed.

'Sure thing. Maybe if there are bushwhackers out there they ain't seen us yet,' Tom said as he checked his Colt.

'They've seen us,' Adams snorted.

'Then how come they ain't done nothing?'

Gene Adams pulled his gloves tight over his hands.

'Because it was getting dark I guess. They couldn't be certain of getting us in the half-light.'

Happy slid from his saddle. He sucked in his cigarette smoke deeply as he squared up to Adams.

'If you're right, Gene, what we gonna do? We can't stay out here waiting for them critters to attack.'

Gene Adams rested a hand upon the man's shoulder.

'I figure a couple of us better go take us a closer look at the fort, Happy.'

The wrangler felt a cold shiver rising

up his spine as he began to understand exactly what Gene Lon Adams meant.

★　★　★

Fortunately for the two Bar 10 men, as they began riding towards Fort Boone the bright moon managed to get itself tangled up in a large black cloud causing an obscurity that served as their only shield. It was a mere two miles or so to the fortress but Gene Adams had decided it was safer to ride than crawl. Tom Conners rode at his side; both of the skilled horsemen knew that they had to move as fast as their mounts could take them before the moon showed its face again and made them a pair of sitting ducks for whoever might be lurking out there in the thousand or more hiding-places. It had been a tough decision for the rancher to make but he had chosen to leave Happy Summers guarding the herd with Larry Baker, whilst taking Tom on his speedy cutting horse with him. Whether it was the correct decision or not the rancher had no time to worry. Adams leaned far over the neck of his charging mare and urged the animal on as he kept one eye glued to the cloudy sky. Tom kept pace with the tall chestnut as they sped along the narrow gulch trying to outrun the reappearance of the moon.

The two horses thundered down the pass unhindered by anything or anyone. Then the ground before them suddenly became brighter as the blue moonlight bathed their route once more. Glancing over his shoulder the rancher could see the new moon glaring down over them. Adams rocked his entire body in trying to get the mare to increase her speed as he caught sight of the open gates of the fort ahead of them. Tom drew level with him and looked over at his boss as they rode at breakneck pace. Adams had never seen fear in the young cowboy's eyes until now. It was etched into every muscle of his face as he tried to keep up with the bigger horse.

Then it started.

Blazing bullets criss-crossed before them, sending deafening echoes bouncing off the surrounding hills. Within fifty yards of the fort Adams's worst fears became reality as the small cutting horse crashed into the ground next to him, sending the young cowboy spilling head over heels.

Adams dragged his chestnut to a halt and paused for an instant as he looked back at the prone body of Tom Conners lying in the soft sand just off the trail. There was no let-up in the furious onslaught of flying lead which was spattering the ground between them. Yet even as he felt the heat of the bullets flying past him, Adams held his horse in check until he saw Tom's dazed body moving up on to all fours. Then he spurred the mare.

Gene Adams rode through the hailstone of lead until he reached his stunned friend, who was staggering about unaware of the bullets trying to claim his life. Adams leaned down, grabbed Tom's arm and swung him up on to his saddle cantle before spurring off again. Riding as he had never ridden before, the rancher steered his trusty mount straight through the open gateway of Fort Boone before reining up.

8

The two cowboys stared in horror at one another as the deafening sound of gunfire filled the air around the chuck-wagon. Happy Summers grabbed his reins and threw himself up into his saddle. He steadied his mount as a bewildered Larry Baker secured the water barrel. Clutching tightly at his reins Happy sucked the last of the smoke from his cigarette before spitting it out on to the dry ground. The sound of bullets echoed off the gulch walls, stirring the restless longhorns behind the chuck-wagon into a startled bellowing. Both men glared back at the herd woefully. The massive beasts were nervous but not nearly as much as the two cowboys. When cattle get edgy they also got mighty dangerous and both wranglers knew it.

Larry Baker climbed up on to his

driver's seat, released the brake-pole and wrapped the massive leather reins around his arms, holding the team in check. The moon now shone in a sky unhindered by clouds sending its brilliant light down across the arid scene.

'Did they make it, Happy?' Larry called out to his friend as they both looked out at the flashing venom of rifle-bullet traces ahead of them.

'Beats me. All I know for certain is that there are gunmen on top of them ridges,' Happy replied grimly.

'What we gonna do?' Larry yelled out as he fought with his team of four nervous horses.

Happy turned his buckskin around and gently spurred it until it was below his friend's perch on the wagon-seat.

'Reckon we got only one choice, Larry.'

'Do just as Gene told us?'

'That's about it.' Happy swung the horse around until it faced the herd. 'When I get these steers stampeding, you crack that whip and head for the fort. If'n we get lucky we just might make it.'

'Whoever is firing them carbines ain't aiming at us, Happy.'

'They will, Larry. They will.'

Larry watched as his friend sank his spurs into his mount and galloped off towards the restless longhorns. He knew if anyone could get forty nervous steers charging in the same direction at once it was Happy Summers.

The burly cowboy rode far better than he had ever been able to walk and soon found himself at the rear of the angry snorting beasts. Waving his saddle rope around above his Stetson in the night air, and shouting at the confused creatures, the wrangler soon had the steers moving towards the wagon in the direction of the distant fort. Sounds of remote shots still filled the air as the solitary cowboy drove the startled cattle on towards the gulch, which was the only route between the fort and themselves. This was the first time

Happy had ever created a stampede and it went against everything he had ever been taught. Cowboys risked their lives trying to prevent stampedes and yet, as he whistled and yelled at the frightened steers, he knew this was what Adams had told him to do if he heard any gunfire.

The forty longhorn steers charged past the chuck-wagon and it began to rock as the ground vibrated beneath its wheels. Larry screamed and cracked his bullwhip over the heads of his anxious team. They stormed forward, hauling their heavy load over the uneven ground as Larry gritted his teeth and steered them after the rampaging cattle.

Dust rose like a whirlwind from the hoofs of the charging cattle. Thick choking dust. Yet for the pair of wranglers there could not be enough blinding dust, this night.

Happy rode after the animals as if possessed by the Devil and used every ounce of his skill keeping the group together in one mighty mass of rampaging muscle.

The deadly horns of the steers flashed in the eerie moonlight as the creatures raced across the dry-baked ground. The dust which rose from the beasts began to veil the wagon as it drew level with the right flank of the longhorns. Charging straight ahead, Larry tried to keep his team aiming at the fort while avoiding all the panic-stricken animals which charged alongside his vehicle. The broad leather reins tore into the flesh of his hands as he battled with his team of galloping horses, yet Larry felt no pain. Fear had somehow dulled his senses to everything except the sound of rifles above them.

Louder and louder the sound of the gunfire grew.

Only the dust which rose like a plague of locusts protected the two cowboys as they forced their charges closer to the fort.

Then the bullets were no longer mere echoes, but aimed towards them. Red traces of deadly lead zipped through the air about them from the high ridges. Steers fell heavily into the ground as unaimed shots brought them down. Chaos reigned amid the carnage but they continued on and on. As Happy leaned over the neck of his galloping buckskin mount he could just make out the flashing rifle barrels high above them through the blinding dust. With the cunning of an expert horseman, he wrapped himself around the neck of his charging horse, knowing the snipers would not be able to spot him.

Larry gritted his teeth and drove his team on in the wake of the herd. Bullets bounced off the high metal wagon-bows above his head yet he continued whipping the team. Now there was no chance to change his mind. He had only one chance of seeing another sun-up. He had to keep going and keep praying. Now the dust was no longer a choking nuisance but a shield of protection.

At that exact moment, five miles to the south of the stampeding herd, Tomahawk and Johnny Puma had just reached the inhospitable Sugar Loaf Mesa. The two riders pulled their lathered up mounts to a weary stop and sat motionless in their saddles listening to the noise of gunfire ringing out across the desolate prairie.

'Hear that, old-timer?' Johnny said angrily as he vainly stood in his stirrups staring out at the moonlit horizon before them. 'We are too late. Gene and the boys are caught up in a damn battle out there.'

'Sounds like they've been dry-gulched, son,' Tomahawk said calmly.

'Come on, old-timer,' Johnny urged as a weathered hand grabbed at his bridle and stopped him racing off towards the direful noise.

Tomahawk dismounted and removed his hat before dropping it on the ground at his horse's feet.

'Water your horse, Johnny.'

The young man gazed in astonishment at his pal who was calmly unscrewing a canteen and pouring the liquid into his upturned Stetson.

'Are you crazy? We gotta get there and help them. Now.'

Tomahawk stood before the pinto pony and looked up at the handsome features of his distraught friend.

'The horses are beat, boy. Get off this pony and give it a drink.'

'There ain't no time . . . '

Tomahawk raised his voice.

'Get off the horse, Johnny. Without water and at least an hour's rest, these critters won't carry us another mile before their hearts burst.'

Johnny Puma gritted his teeth and stared hard down at his friend.

'In an hour we might lose four of our best pals, Tomahawk.'

Tomahawk nodded. 'Listen to an old man. Get off your horse, boy. Don't act like a hothead this time. We gotta do this right otherwise we ain't gonna be no help to Gene and the boys.'

Johnny swallowed his pride and felt confused as he threw himself down on to the hard dry ground beside Tomahawk.

The old man handed the canteen to him, then moved back to his own horse and began removing the saddle.

'An hour?' Johnny asked as he took off his hat and dropped it down before his pinto.

Tomahawk grunted as he dragged the heavy saddle off his horse's back and rested it on the ground between them.

'You gotta realize one thing, boy. These horses of ours are faithful critters with hardly no brains at all. They'll keep galloping as long as we keep jabbing the spurs into their flesh. They'll keep going at full steam until they drop. Why? Because they figure we know what we're doing. They kinda expect us to be smarter than they is.'

Johnny poured the remainder of the canteen's contents into his Stetson and then turned to look at the old crumpled features of Tomahawk.

'I guess you must be right but the sound of them bullets is making me a tad edgy.'

'As long as them bullets are being fired, I figure there's a fight going on. When the shooting stops, then we got cause to be a mite worried, Johnny.'

Johnny Puma threw his stirrup over the seat of his saddle and began untying the cinch strap. His horse was soaked in sweat as he pulled the heavy saddle and blanket off its back. Steam drifted into the moonlight.

'Has Gene got an hour, Tomahawk?' Johnny asked, as he dropped the saddle on to the ground.

There was no answer.

9

As bullets blasted unceasingly away at the fort and the charging herd of longhorns, a muted confusion swirled over the dust-enveloped creatures. Half the steers were carrying lead from the bushwhackers' rifles as they thundered past the open gateway leaving a cloud of impenetrable dust in their wake. The chuck-wagon somehow made it through the open gates of Fort Boone only seconds after Happy Summers had thrown himself from his buckskin mount and rushed for cover beside the silent Gene Adams behind the wooden walls. Larry Baker pulled the brake-pole back with every ounce of his remaining strength, then reached beneath the driver's seat and hauled his Winchester up into his bleeding hands. He had no time to think as a familiar voice sounded from the shadows behind him.

'Get over here, Larry.'

Larry climbed quickly down from the wagon and ran towards Gene Adams's distinctive tones.

Falling from exhaustion at the tall rancher's feet, Larry gave a sigh of relief as he felt his back being tapped with a pointed toecap.

'Get up, Larry. You ain't dead yet.' Gene Adams held out a helping hand and pulled the cowboy back on to his feet.

Larry staggered but was comforted to be beside the stalwart Adams, who was clutching one of his gold-plated pistols in his gloved left hand.

'What's happening, Gene?'

'Ain't quite figured it out yet, Larry,' Adams responded honestly, looking carefully through the gap between the large door and the high wooden wall.

The young wrangler stared around at the shadows and the moonlit scene within the walls of the fort. Suddenly the true horror of their situation hit him. There were bodies littered about the parade-ground and buildings. It was evident that none of the troopers who had remained at the fort were still in the land of the living.

'What the hell is happening?' Larry's voice broke as panic rose within his breast.

Gripping the youngster's shoulder, Adams tried to make light of their predicament.

'You noticed the dead cavalry, I see.'

'Who would wanna kill an entire garrison, Gene?'

'Wish I had an answer, Larry.'

'Why would anyone . . . ?'

'For some reason there are a mess of folks out there who are a little ornery, Larry boy,' Adams replied. He turned and stared hard into the younger man's face. 'I reckon they've got plenty of ammunition, though, by the way they keep shooting.'

Larry rubbed his sweating face with a shaking hand.

'What they got against these soldier-boys and us, Gene?'

Adams frowned. 'Something tells me that I'm the one they want.'

'What?'

'I'm the one who got sent the telegram. Remember?' Adams watched as the dry sand outside the fort continued to be churned up by their hidden enemy's bullets.

'All this killing just to get you?' Larry felt his stomach turn as he thought about the situation.

'It don't figure, Gene,' Happy Summers said. He began rolling another cigarette in his clumsy hands.

'Maybe not to a sane man like you, Happy.' Adams gritted his teeth and squinted hard out at the distant flashes of carbine fire.

'We've just run into some kinda war,' Happy said. He ran his tongue along the gum of the cigarette paper.

'What you looking at, Gene?' Larry stepped to the man's side.

Adams pointed at the ground ten feet

away from the open gates as bullets tore up its friable surface.

'Whoever they are, they ain't got the range from where they're holed up, boys.'

'So to get the range . . . ' Larry began.

'They gotta break cover and come a tad closer.' Adams finished the youngster's sentence for him. 'Break out the extra carbines, Larry. You'll find them under the chuck-box in the wagon-boot, along with a dozen boxes of ammunition.'

Happy edged his way closer to the two men.

'We lost the herd, Gene.'

Adams shook his head.

'They'll stop running when they reach the river.'

'Where's Tom, Gene?' Happy asked, trying to focus his eyes in the annoying moonlight.

Adams pointed behind him to a darkened corner of the fort where the young injured cowboy lay propped up against the wall.

'Tom got himself busted up, Happy.'

'They shoot him?'

'Nope. They killed his horse and he took a real bad fall.' Adams leaned around the edge of the massive door and fired a few shots back at their hidden enemy. He knew it was pointless but it made him feel better to let his enemies know someone was still alive within the fort.

'How bad a fall, Gene?' Happy swallowed deeply before striking a match across the wall and putting its flame to his cigarette.

Adams stared into Happy's eyes as Larry headed off towards the chuck-wagon.

'Real bad, Happy.'

The usually jovial cowboy went to kneel down beside the stricken man.

'Tom? You hear me. Tom?'

Tom Conners forced a smile as he gazed through moist blurred eyes at his pal.

'You got the makings, Happy?'

Happy pulled out his tobacco-pouch from his shirt-pocket and began rolling one of his two paper 'specials' for the pale man who seemed unable to move as the smoke from his own cigarette stung his eyes. Happy placed the cigarette between Tom's dry lips, struck a match and touched the flame to the end of the smoke. Tom inhaled and smiled at his pal thankfully.

'Better?' Happy settled himself beside the wrangler.

'Reckon so, Happy.' Tom nodded as he inhaled the smoke deep into his lungs and felt the pain ease. 'I'm kinda winded by the fall. Never felt so bad before.'

'Anything broke?'

'Reckon so.' Tom allowed the smoke to drift through his teeth as he turned his head towards Happy. 'Funny thing is, I've been thrown by mustangs and had all sorts of bronchos kick the tar outa me in the past but I ain't never felt like this.'

Happy watched as the burning end of

Tom's cigarette began to touch his lips. It was as if Tom could not tell he was being burned. Happy removed the butt from his friend's mouth and rammed it into the sand beside them.

'You broke your arms, Tom?'

Tom smiled again as the final traces of smoke filtered through his teeth.

'I'm gonna have me a sleep, Happy.'

Happy removed his jacket, rolled it up and placed it beneath Tom's head. Then he straightened up and moved back to Gene Adams.

'Tom needs a doctor, Gene.'

Adams sighed. 'Help me close these darn gates, Happy.'

'What about Tom?' Happy felt a knot in his craw which kept twisting like a knife. The taste of terror was something the wrangler had never encountered before. Even spitting could not take its poison from the man's palate.

'Ain't nothing we can do, son. Only pray.' Gene Adams thought about the young men he had brought here to this lethal place. Men whom he felt he had betrayed. Then he thought about Johnny Puma and Tomahawk. Leaving them and their undoubted skills back on the Bar 10 might have been his last mistake.

Adams and Happy slowly closed the massive gates and secured them.

★ ★ ★

The Wolf raised an arm and his men instantly ceased firing. His cold eyes stared out from beneath his long matted hair as he strolled down off the highest point of the tall ridge towards the small camp. He had never been what anyone might have referred to as handsome before his capture but now he seemed almost devoid of anything close to human features. Five years had seen his face disappear beneath the never-ending growth of hair. His beard had reached his chest and his hair hung limply from his head. The features that still remained visible were pock-marked with sores which scarred and deformed.

Yet for all his ugliness, the eyes still burned like two Roman candles on the Fourth of July.

Only his clothing bore any connection with the man he had once been: well-tailored clothes which his men had kept for him during his incarceration. Now they hung on his frame, another reminder of why he had hated Gene Adams for so long, with such venom. The Wolf was no mere outlaw, but a force of total evil bent on killing Gene Adams as slowly and as painfully as possible. He had dispatched over two dozen soldiers to an early grave already just to make his plan succeed. Now he had the Bar 10 man exactly where he wanted him. Five years of crazed planning had somehow fallen into place like a child's jigsaw puzzle.

It had been so easy. So utterly simple.

The outlaws moved behind the Wolf as he reached the blazing camp-fire they had lit in the cover of the gulch, far away from the eyes of his enemy.

When the Wolf sat down next to the

flames, they all copied him. Gathered around the fire, the Wolf stared at the faces of his men. Now reduced to a mere dozen or so, they still hovered like vultures for his next orders.

Even after five years of hard labour, going half-crazy in iron shackles, he could still do something they seemed unable to do successfully, he was still capable of thought. His brain, although twisted by savage retribution, could plan and execute cunning schemes.

He was still the Wolf and they merely his pack.

These were cowering outlaws, afraid of what their master had become and yet unwilling to stray far from his side. Hanging his head as if in exhaustion the Wolf mumbled to himself under his breath. None of the assembled gathering could or would do anything which might bring his wrath upon them and away from the cowboys they had trapped within the fort.

At last the Wolf looked up at them and began laughing. It was not the laugh of a man who had seen or heard something humorous but more the cruel laughter of a man who took pleasure in his own depravity.

'We did it, boys. We trapped the bastard.'

'But he's inside the fort, Wolf,' one of the men said in a confused tone. 'He could hole up there for weeks. I don't get it, we could have killed them as they rode in but you wanted them to get into the fort. Why?'

'Why?' The Wolf shook his head as if pitying his mindless followers.

'Yep,' another of the men added. 'They could hold out in the fort for weeks, Wolf.'

'Not with a poisoned well.' The Wolf laughed loudly as he remembered how he and his gang had watched the small detachment of cavalry leaving the fort on their weekly patrol. The Wolf had waited a few hours before riding to the fort. He lowered his head and began to chuckle as he recalled how easily he and his men had ridden in through the gates of Fort Boone. They had gone unchallenged by the inept troops as they had asked for and were granted access.

How easy it had been for his well-armed men to spread themselves out within the fort and begin their killing. It seemed as if none of the soldiers had ever even considered that white men could be the enemy.

They had learned the folly of that reasoning. During the attack he had lost a few of his men to the soldiers, who had managed to get off a few lucky shots, but it did not alter his resolve. To him, these were casualties of a greater war. His war with the man known as Gene Adams.

The Wolf picked up a bottle of rye from beside him, tugged out its cork with what remained of his teeth and spat it away before starting to consume its contents. Every swallow brought the colour of those sad soldiers' blood back into his eager memory. The Wolf had ensured his men killed every living creature belonging to the fort besides the troopers. Every steer, every horse and even the chickens and hogs in the outside corrals and stables. Nothing of use to Adams and his cowboys remained at the remote garrison.

The Wolf watched as some of his men began preparing a meal with the food they had taken from the fort. The Wolf had ensured nothing remotely edible remained within the larders and cellars of Fort Boone. Piled high around the Wolf's camp was every provision from Fort Boone, from every salted side of beef and bacon to the cases of whiskey and beer.

Even if it all rotted on the ground within their makeshift camp, he did not care. As long as Adams and his cowboys could not eat it, he was content. All the Bar 10 cowboys had to eat and drink was carried in their prairie schooner. A barrel of water and a chuck-box full of flour and salt would not last them long, the Wolf mused.

'I want three sentries,' the Wolf ordered waving the bottle around. 'I want you to make sure nobody tries to come to their rescue. Nobody gets in and nobody gets out. I'm gonna see Adams beg for me to slit his throat, boys.'

Suddenly they were all laughing.

10

Darkness still dominated the Texas landscape as clouds swept across the sky above the two riders' heads. Vainly the moon appeared every few minutes giving the pair a brief glimpse of where they had found themselves. The sound of shooting, which had guided them for the first two miles, had ceased over an hour earlier. Johnny Puma had trailed the more experienced Tomahawk to this flat dry place. Only Tomahawk could have located the last place where Gene Adams's herd of longhorns had rested before heading for the fort.

Johnny Puma pulled up his reins and stopped the pinto short as he watched Tomahawk dismounting a few yards ahead of him. The old man moved close to the ground as he studied its tell-tale signs. Signs which his years of living with Indians had etched into his soul.

Johnny threw his right leg over the saddle horn and slid down on to the moonlit ground. He held the bridle of his pony tight as he watched the old man moving slowly over the hard ground.

As Tomahawk straightened up, Johnny strode to his side.

'Well?'

'I don't like what I see, boy.' Tomahawk sighed, rubbing his beard with his hands.

'Did Gene come this way?'

Tomahawk nodded.

'They drove the herd through here OK.'

'Then what's eating at you?' Johnny was as nervous as his pony as the moon once more disappeared behind a black cloud above them.

'Gene rode off with Tom first over there.' Tomahawk pointed at the direction their friends had taken. 'I can't figure out why Happy stampeded the herd directly at the fort though.'

'Are you sure Happy stampeded the

herd, Tomahawk?' Johnny removed his Stetson and wiped his brow on his sleeve. It was a strange feeling that chilled the young cowboy's bones as he tried to work out what must have occurred.

'Yep. Gene and Tom went yonder and then a short while afterwards, Happy got the herd frenzied up and charged them straight through the gulch. The chuck-wagon headed off with the herd.'

'Why would they split up?' Johnny shook his head as he felt the lack of sleep beginning to weary him.

'Why didn't they just drive the herd straight at the fort?' Tomahawk rubbed his neck before his keen nose began to get a hint of an aroma on the cold night air. 'You smell that?'

Johnny inhaled deeply.

'I smell carcasses, old-timer.'

Tomahawk spat at the ground and stared hard down through the long gulch, wishing his eyes were twenty years younger.

'Something's dead, all right.'

'Maybe it's just a few steers lying out there in the gulch,' Johnny wished aloud, hoping his worst fears were nothing more than a tired brain attempting to understand something no sane mind could ever fully grasp.

'We better be as cautious as Gene was, boy,' Tomahawk said solemnly.

Johnny stood holding his reins thoughtfully as he looked up at the sky, now patchy with rain clouds. The moon seemed like a lantern whose wick was being lowered and then raised, its light never constant, never allowing the two cowboys to focus for more than a few fleeting seconds at a stretch.

'The gunfire stopped an awful long while ago, old-timer.'

'Sure enough did.' Tomahawk stared out at the distant fort at least two miles away through the narrow gulch. He cursed his inability to see more than its crude shape whenever the moonlight hit its towers.

'I never did cotton on to gulches, Tomahawk,' Johnny said.

'Me neither. Ambush country,' the older man added.

'Yep.'

'We gonna ride down through that gulch, boy?'

'Nope.' Johnny gathered up his reins and moved back to the neck of his pinto. 'I reckon we oughta circle the hills, just in case them dry-gulchers are still awake and primed.'

'Must have been a turkey shoot.' Tomahawk spat angrily once more at the ground.

'Gene is smart. He'd have ridden his chestnut mare faster than any bullet could travel, old man.'

Tomahawk walked silently back towards his waiting quarter-horse and grabbed at the saddle horn before pushing his left boot-toe into the stirrup and hauling himself up. He knew Gene Adams was no fool but even he could not imagine anyone making it safely through the narrow gulch whilst under fire from the high ridges.

'Right or left?'

Johnny mounted his pony and steadied it as he studied their limited choices.

'We oughta ride around to the left, I figure.'

Tomahawk nodded, tapped his spurs gently into the sides of his mount and started off towards the dark shadows where Johnny was pointing. Standing in his stirrups, Johnny allowed his pinto pony to trail the more experienced rider. Now the black clouds passed over the moon, cascading their route into blackness once more.

Tomahawk turned his collar up to protect his ears from the biting breeze as his partner looked heavenward at the sky, its light now totally covered. Not even one star could penetrate the gloom above their heads.

'Can you see where you're headed, old-timer?' Johnny asked as he drew level with the black horse.

'When you gets as old as me, you can see better in the dark than in the daylight, sonny,' Tomahawk bragged.

'Yeah?'

'Yep. Anyway, the darker it gets the better I like it,' Tomahawk sniffed.

Looking around them as they travelled, Johnny ran his tongue over his cracked lips.

'You figure we can get the drop on them varmints?'

'I sure hope so.'

They had a long ride ahead of them. A ride which would take them well clear of the gulch and its bushwhackers. As they steered their horses down around the tall ridge they knew every passing minute might mean the difference between life and death to their friends.

11

Gene Adams had tried to make the injured cowboy as comfortable as possible inside the old chuck-wagon. Tom Conners was young, but old enough to know when things were seriously wrong. As Larry, Happy and Gene had carefully picked him up from the hard ground and carried him to the wagon he had felt nothing at all. No pain whatsoever. Tom knew he was busted up badly enough to be in agony but there was no feeling anywhere in his body any more.

During the hours since he had crashed to the ground from his felled cutting horse, his body had slowly begun to go dead. Straight after the fall, Tom had managed to get to his feet and throw himself up behind Gene Adams's saddle cantle, yet, after reaching the fort, his legs had buckled beneath him.

Shortly afterwards, his arms had refused to obey even the most simple of his commands. Paralysis had crept up him from his toes like a numbing fog which left everything in its wake lifeless. Tom had watched his chest heaving for air beneath the low light of the lantern strung above him for nearly an hour. His head seemed filled with a buzzing sound like a nest of angry hornets determined to keep him awake.

Yet as he lay inside the semi-darkness of the wagon, staring up at the canvas stretched across the metal bows, it seemed as if only his neck was capable of still moving. Watching the wind shaking the well-tied-down canvas, Tom Conners wondered what was happening to him.

It was like a nightmare but he knew he was wide awake.

Tom had seen wranglers kicked so hard by steers and mustangs they could not walk for weeks. He himself had broken more bones than he cared to remember in his days in the saddle, but that had always hurt. Pain had always been part of the overall picture of being a cowboy. Real bad pain.

Where was the pain? Tom screwed his eyes up and tried to make something move. Anything. A finger, a toe. Anything. Gasping in frustration he stared down at his motionless body and felt a tear trickle from the corner of his right eye. He could feel it running slowly over his cheek and down his neck but when it fell on to his chest, there was no sensation.

Tom began to find that even taking in air became more and more difficult as he lay where his pals had left him. Yet there still was no pain. It was as if he could feel nothing below his neck.

Had he broken his neck? Tom began to panic as the enormity of the question raced through his fevered brain.

For the first time in his life, Tom Conners was scared.

★ ★ ★

Happy Summers puffed on his cigarette as he followed Gene Adams up a narrow ladder into the west tower of the fort. When they reached the covered tower they were met by yet another corpse.

'How many damn bodies are there, Gene?' Happy asked.

'I've counted well over twenty so far, Happy,' Adams replied grimly. 'Three of them weren't troopers though.'

'I don't get it.'

Gene Adams leaned on the wall and stared out at the darkness before them and at the rain which was beginning to fall from the black sky.

'I figure these soldiers let a real big bunch of outlaws or the like in through the gates, Happy. Maybe they lied and said they were hunters or something and needed supplies. I can only guess what happened next — but the result was a massacre. This was carefully planned though. These men were executed to satisfy the lust of someone truly evil.'

'Planned?' Happy found it hard to comprehend anyone planning such a brutal venture.

'Yeah. Planned down to the last detail.' Adams rubbed his face as they moved to the corner of the tower and looked down into the silent corrals below.

'My eyes are a tad sore, Gene. Am I seeing what I think I'm seeing?' Happy sucked on his cigarette, being careful to shield the red tip of his smoke from the sights of a sniper.

'Every damn animal has been slaughtered, Happy,' Adams swore angrily. 'Every steer, horse and hog. Dead. These people have killed everything.'

'The entire garrison of cavalry?' Happy gasped.

'Nope. Major Frank Bellamy ain't amongst the dead. Sergeant Flynn ain't here either.' Adams breathed heavily. 'I figure about a dozen of the troopers are missing. Probably out on a patrol.'

'Luckily for them.'

'Yep. Luckily for them,' Adams concurred.

Happy shook his head as he followed the rancher along the wooden parapet to the next tower. There seemed to be a trooper's body every few feet, lying where they had been shot. It was a gruesome sight.

'Thank God it's raining, Happy,' Adams said as they reached the next tower.

'It does kinda keep the smell down,' Happy gulped.

Just then a rain-sodden Larry Baker came rushing up the ladder into the tower where his two pals were standing. Beating the rain from his hat against his chaps, the young man moved close to Adams.

'We gotta lot of trouble, Gene.'

'More trouble, Larry?' Adams gritted his teeth as he stared down at the cowboy before him.

'The well is poisoned,' Larry explained.

'Are you sure?' Happy grabbed his

119

friend's shoulder.

'Dead sure.' Larry replaced his Stetson on his head and watched the faces of his companions.

Gene Adams stretched up to his full height and rested a hand against a wooden upright as he stared out into the rain and the darkness.

'How much water we got left in the wagon barrel?'

'Less than a quarter, Gene,' Larry replied.

Adams stood studying the scene, as his eyes gradually adjusted to the darkness.

'I got me an idea, Happy.'

'An idea?'

Adams nodded. 'Yep. An idea which might just make them bushwhackers a mite confused when the sun comes up.'

'What kinda idea, Gene?' Larry asked eagerly.

'First things first,' Adams began. 'I want you boys to go down and take the lid off the water-barrel so this rain will top it up. Then try and find anything you can around the fort which will catch as much water as possible.'

'Sure enough,' Happy said as he started down the ladder.

'What about your plan?' Larry asked as he stepped on to the top rung of the ladder.

'First things first.' Adams waved him away and brooded.

12

Gene Adams walked through the rain and stood silently beside the chuck-wagon. Somewhere out there beyond the fort walls birds were beginning to greet a new day as if oblivious to the constant downpour. The Fort Boone parade-ground was now nothing more than a three-inch-deep lake of mud. Adams hoped this day might be better than the previous hours of darkness. At least the aroma of death had now gone, beaten into submission by nature's purification. He watched as the rain ran from his wide hat-brim and fell in a never-ending stream before his face. For the first time in all his days, Adams wondered if he would survive to see another Texan sunset. Without his two most trustworthy and reliable friends, Tomahawk and Johnny, at his side, it seemed doubtful.

The parade-ground was covered in buckets, catching the precious water. He leaned over the edge of the water-barrel strapped to the side of the wagon, and looked down into it. Now half-full he prayed the rain would continue long enough to fill it. With the fort well poisoned, Adams knew they wouldn't last long if or when the sun showed its face. It got hotter than hell in this part of Texas.

Happy and Larry came towards him exhausted and soaked after completing his instructions. Neither man seemed capable of lasting another hour, let alone the day. Like himself, they were totally worn out.

'Done it?' Adams asked the two cowboys.

'We done it but I can't figure out why you wanted us to do it, Gene.' Larry coughed from beneath his sodden Stetson.

'You given each one a carbine?' Adams checked.

Happy nodded. 'We slid a fully

loaded carbine under each of their arms.'

'Just like you told us,' Larry added, trying to appear far braver than the rancher had ever expected either of them to be.

Adams moved to the two men and rested a hand upon each of their shoulders.

'Good.'

Happy and Larry watched as the tall rancher strode slowly across the parade-ground, through the ceaseless downpour towards the officers' building, where a solitary wood-stove burned beneath the Bar 10 coffee-pot.

'I'm gonna make us a pot of real strong Java, boys,' Adams called back over his shoulder.

The two young cowboys huddled together beside the chuck-wagon watching the big man amble up on to the boardwalk and into the building before speaking to one another.

'It don't make no sense. No sense at all, Larry,' Happy said quietly to his pal, thinking of what they had done during the past couple of hours.

'It must make sense. We just ain't as smart as Gene is.' Larry cleared his throat as the first rays of the new day began to lighten up the dark brooding sky above them.

'I don't like it,' Happy moaned.

'Neither do I, but Gene's got a plan.' Larry moved to the front of the chuck-wagon and pulled the canvas away from the frame to look inside at the injured Tom who was sleeping at last.

'How is he?' Happy asked his pal reluctantly, afraid of hearing bad news.

'Tom is hanging in there but . . . ' Larry's voice faded as he saw Tom's head move.

'Gene said he reckons Tom might have busted his neck,' Happy mumbled.

Larry replaced the canvas flap and nodded.

'Yep.'

'Is he gonna die?' Happy heard his words trip from his mouth hesitantly.

'Reckon we are all gonna die sometime today, Happy.' Larry smiled. 'Even Gene ain't smart enough to prevent that.'

Happy sighed in agreement and cast an eye over his friend's shoulder up at the fort walls and at their handiwork.

Both men looked up at the wooden towers and along the parapets where they had propped every one of the dead soldiers just as Gene Adams had instructed them to do. Each of the bodies appeared to be armed with a fully loaded carbine carefully tied with rawhide to the lifeless limbs. Neither cowboy had ever touched a dead person before and it frightened them to dwell too deeply on their actions.

An army of ghosts now manned the walls of Fort Boone in an unearthly silence above the weary cowboys. Unlike the Bar 10 cowboys, these troopers were now immune to the lethal bullets which had already captured their souls, sending them to a better place. Now only the bodies remained, empty shells where once living, breathing men had existed. Now they were propped in a deathly sentry duty, devoid of fear.

It was an eerie sight which neither man could comprehend, yet they knew the tired Bar 10 rancher must have something up his sleeve. Adams was cunning.

As the new day quietly began Adams had given his young Bar 10 cowboys a fighting chance by creating an army upon the fort walls.

Whoever was out there might just be tempted to waste valuable lead by shooting at figures they had already killed. The more ammunition used on the dead soldiers, the less could be used upon them. It seemed a vain hope, but at least it was a chance of confusing their mysterious enemy. An enemy who would stop at nothing to achieve his goals.

Would it work?

Adams stepped out from the officers' quarters carrying a pot of coffee in one hand and a few tin mugs in the other. He waited beneath the wooden over-hang.

'Come and drink this, boys,' he ordered.

The two cowboys waded through the mud towards the rancher.

'We're in a real bad fix, boys,' Adams admitted as he handed the cups to the two men.

'We've been in worse fixes, Gene,' Happy said, shaking off his hat before hanging it on his gun hammer.

'I don't think so, Happy.' Adams blew out heavily trying to find yet another second wind. He was dog-tired but knew that if he gave in, these two youngsters would be helpless.

'I hope this coffee is real strong, Gene, 'cos I'm tuckered out,' Larry said.

'Two cups of this and you won't be able to blink for a week, son.' Adams grinned as he rested the heavy pot down on the boards beside them before blowing at the steaming beverage in his gloved hand.

'Why have we given a bunch of dead troopers loaded repeating rifles, Gene?' Larry finally found the courage to ask.

Adams sipped at the strong drink and felt its immediate effect.

'Whoever is out there is after my hide, Larry. That I can bet good money on. Whoever it is is crazed by vengeance. Only a crazy man bent on revenge would risk so much for so little gain and would go to so much trouble to trap anyone like he's managed to trap me. You boys are stuck because you're with me. I guess the idea of putting them dead soldier boys up on the walls with rifles does seem a tad strange but just think what that crazy varmint and his henchmen are gonna think when they wake up to see all them troopers.'

Happy swallowed his coffee and bent down to refill his tin cup.

'Why are their rifles loaded, Gene?'

'I figure you boys are young and nimble enough to scoot around the walls squeezing the triggers on those carbines.' Adams raised an eyebrow as he looked at his men.

'I get it.' Larry laughed.

Adams gazed across at the chuck-wagon as the morning light began to touch its drenched canvas.

'Fix a cup of coffee for Tom, Happy. I'll take it to him.'

★　★　★

Johnny Puma and Tomahawk had made slow progress through the tortuous terrain below the dry ridges south of the long winding gulch that led to the fort. The pair pulled their horses to a halt, dismounted and slowly tried to work out where exactly they were.

Nothing had travelled this way for a very long time judging by the state of the ground. Only the continuous rain had left any tracks here, the older man declared.

'Where in tarnation are we, old-timer?' Johnny asked, taking a long drink from his canteen before handing it to his partner.

'If we head up through these rocks, I figure we oughta come out close to them sharp-shooting bastards, Johnny.' Tomahawk scratched his beard as he felt the rain stinging his skin beneath his drenched clothing.

Johnny looked at the ominous rocks gleaming in the morning light as rain poured over their smooth surfaces. They were big and offered no way through for their mounts. Slowly the young cowboy turned and faced the bedraggled Tomahawk.

'We'll have to leave the horses here.'

'Reckon so,' Tomahawk agreed.

'You figure you can make it over these boulders, old-timer?'

Tomahawk narrowed his eyes and glared up at the youngster.

'I could hop over these little pebbles, you young maverick.'

Johnny checked his guns carefully, then turned to face the rocks, trying to work out a navigable route up the rugged heights before returning his attention to his partner.

'You sure look like an old goat, Tomahawk.'

Tomahawk tied their reins to the sparse brush.

'It ain't gonna be an easy climb.'

'Not if this rain keeps on coming down.' Johnny Puma hung a full canteen of water over his shoulder before pulling both their Winchester repeating rifles from their scabbards and handing one to the older man. His face was carved with a determination Tomahawk had seldom witnessed before.

'You ready, boy?' Tomahawk asked as he trailed the long-limbed youth through the narrow gaps between the rocks before they began to climb up over its slippery surface.

Neither man spoke again as they started their ascent. They now had to climb over rocks which felt like greased panes of glass beneath their high-heeled boots. Even on a dry day, this climb would have been treacherous but as the rain water continuously streamed down over the smooth rocks, defying the two cowboys to maintain contact with them, it became a fight for survival. Every inch they managed to climb was bitterly contested by the never-ending flow of water. Johnny paused twenty feet above the ground and turned to Tomahawk below.

'I can't keep climbing with this rifle in my hand, Tomahawk,' he admitted.

The older man nodded in agreement. They both released their grips on their Winchesters and watched the weapons sliding down the wet rocks before landing next to their horses.

There were no further words between the two. Nothing could describe their innermost trepidation. Every thought was on the task at hand. The slow deliberate climb would take every ounce of their concentration and resolve to complete. Each step was filled with more danger than they could have imagined.

As Johnny tentatively led the way, he began to find his respect for the older cowboy growing. Tomahawk somehow managed to stay with him.

13

The Wolf stood on the very edge of the ridge glaring through the rain to the distant fort. He, unlike his men, had not slept during the night but had spent the time drinking the entire contents of two whiskey bottles, the way most men sucked in fresh air. However much he consumed, it did not appear to make any difference to him. His mind was constantly blurred by the madness only certain creatures ever discover. No amount of alcohol could alter a brain so immersed in its own insanity.

The rain had alerted him to the new day. Continuous rain which had killed the camp-fire and soaked him to his underwear. The Wolf had not made any provision in his ruthless planning for rain and it infuriated him. He had never known it to rain here on the edge of the vast Texan prairie before. Here the sun bleached the bones of all who tried to ignore its power.

Yet it was raining relentlessly.

The Wolf pulled the brim of his hat down over his temples and tried to focus his bloodshot eyes upon the distant vision almost obscured by the never-ending cascade of water droplets. What he thought he saw could not be real, he concluded. The day was young and the light poor.

Nevertheless, the Wolf was worried. Pulling both his Smith & Wesson Schofield .45s from their wet holsters, the Wolf raised them above his head and fired once with each pistol. Without turning he could hear his men coming to life behind him as the noise of his shots reverberated around the rocks.

Casting an eye to his right he watched the sentry, who had been sleeping, jump to his feet in shock. For a brief moment, the Wolf felt like killing the man for not remaining awake at his post. Then he considered the other two sentries who had also been sleeping

136

during the night, unaware of anything. If he killed one, he would have to kill all three. Even the Wolf was not crazy enough to waste three of his men so pointlessly.

Most of his gang gathered around the Wolf as he lowered his weapons back into their holsters.

'What's wrong, Wolf?' one of the men asked.

The Wolf pointed towards Fort Boone.

'Tell me what you see.'

The men all screwed their eyes up trying to see the wooden structure through the driving rain. There was a lot of mumbling amongst their ragged ranks before one croaked:

'I see rifle-barrels glinting.'

The Wolf held the bridge of his nose and angrily snorted out on to the ground a large volume of congested mucus.

'What else?'

'Soldiers,' another voice added from beside him.

The Wolf shrugged. 'You see soldiers?'

There seemed to be a unanimous grunting from his men which confirmed his own sighting. The Wolf moved around in a circle kicking at the wet ground with the toes of his boots. He stopped in the exact spot from where he had started, rested an arm on the shoulder of one of his outlaws and began shaking his head.

'How many soldiers do you see, Raif?'

The man lifted his index finger and counted those figures dotted about the fort walls that were visible from their vantage-point.

'Twenty?'

The Wolf stomped his foot on the ground and squared up to the fort as if it were a living entity.

'You see twenty soldier-boys when there cannot be twenty soldier-boys?' he screamed.

'We killed them all two days ago,' one of the older outlaws declared.

'Correct,' the Wolf boomed as his

crazed eyes flashed about the gang members. 'Now they have somehow come back to life and are upon the walls of the fort again.'

A thin figure moved beside the Wolf and stared at him with ice-cold eyes.

'Maybe the patrol returned during the night, Wolf.'

It was a good suggestion which made the strange man start nodding as he moved across to the three sentries he had awoken only minutes earlier. Shaking as the rain fell from the merciless storm clouds, the trio of men became fearful as their leader drew closer to them. The entire gang became silent as they watched the Wolf pulling both his guns from his holsters and begin toying with them.

'Did the patrol return?' the Wolf asked the three men who knew when to be afraid of their leader. 'I asked you if the patrol came back but you would have had to be awake to have seen that, wouldn't you?'

Looking at one another, the terrified men soon realized none of them had any answers to the simple questions. They had all slept and seen nothing.

Faster than the strike of a diamondback rattler, the Wolf whipped his gun barrels across their faces until each of the men found himself upon his knees in the mud at Wolf's feet. Blood poured from their open wounds as they grovelled around trying to regain their senses. They had no stomach to fight back. The Wolf had always been able to rely upon his men's inability to stand up to him and five years in prison had not changed things one iota.

'If just one of you lazy bastards had kept your damn eyes open we would have seen the patrol returning and been able to cut them down before they reached the fort,' the Wolf growled angrily as he paced back to the main group of outlaws.

'How do we know it is the patrol, Wolf?' an outlaw asked.

The Wolf stared at the blood on his

gun-barrels before sliding them back into his holsters.

'True. Gene Adams might just be playing a game with us.'

'How?' another voice queried.

'Would Adams be so cunning? To use the bodies of dead troopers to fool me?' The Wolf moved around his men once more and then stopped, shaking his head again. 'He must know it's me out here, boys.'

'Adams ain't that smart, Wolf.'

The Wolf began to stare up at the sky and mumble as if trying to make contact with a greater entity, a being who could aid his demented, meticulous plans.

'What's wrong, Wolf?' the thin man asked his leader cautiously.

'It ain't supposed to be raining,' the Wolf said, looking up at the angry clouds as they swirled over their heads.

'What ya mean, Wolf?'

'It ain't meant to rain. I never planned for it to rain.' The Wolf walked back towards their camp, leaving his scabrous bunch of men in his wake. He was mumbling under his breath again and none of his gang liked it. Five years had changed the Wolf in ways none of them felt easy with. He had always been dangerous but now, even to this menagerie of half-wits, he seemed to be totally insane.

14

Happy Summers was the first to notice the line of riders slowly approaching the fort through the driving rain. Each of the dozen or more horsemen, carried a cocked repeating rifle resting on his hip. The raised carbines gave the appearance of lances carried by ancient crusaders.

Adams rushed to the side of the trembling cowboy in the southernmost tower and looked out at the riders. For a moment, the rancher said nothing as he watched the long line of mounted outlaws getting closer and closer. Then his jaw dropped and he felt a cold chill rushing up his spine.

'What is it, Gene?' Happy questioned.

'The Wolf,' Adams muttered slowly as he instinctively drew both his gold-plated Colts from their holsters and rested his gloved wrists on top of the wooden wall.

Happy knew nothing of the Wolf nor the reasons for the animosity between the two men. All he knew was he had never seen the face of his boss looking so grim. So concerned.

'Who is he?'

Adams swallowed deeply, trying to understand how the man he had thought was locked up for ever could possibly be riding towards them.

'The Wolf,' Adams repeated.

Larry Baker ran up the ladder behind the cowboys and rushed to their side.

'Who the heck are they?'

Adams stared up at the sky as if in silent prayer before looking at each of his men in turn.

'If I were to tell you everything I know about that critter, you boys would never sleep again without having nightmares.'

'What are they doing?' Larry questioned as he stood staring at the defiant riders who continued their progress towards them.

'He ain't like normal folks, Larry.' Adams began to wonder whether his attempt to confuse their enemy might just explode in his face. He was not dealing with any normal maniac, this was the Wolf.

Then, a hundred yards from the front wall of Fort Boone, the riders drew in their reins and halted their mounts. Steam rose from the line of animals as they swayed in the pouring rain.

'What we gonna do, Gene?' Happy pleaded for advice.

Adams gripped the man's shoulder and squeezed it gently.

'We hold firm, Happy. We do exactly as I told you earlier. We make them think these dead soldiers are alive.'

'Will they fall for it?'

'The Wolf is crazy enough to fall for anything as long as we do it right,' Gene Adams said, his guns back into their holsters before pulling a Winchester from the arms of one of the dead troopers in the tower.

Happy bent double and ran along the wooden parapet to the far tower where he knelt beside the body of one of the hapless cavalry. Larry waited for his friend to stop before he also ran, crouching, to the centre of the parapet, where he stopped beside another of the posed corpses. Both men waited with eyes on the tall Bar 10 rancher as he primed the rifle in his gloved grip.

Adams leant against an upright and watched the line of motionless outlaws. He had been in many a tight spot but never anything like this. He felt his mouth drying at an alarming rate as he held the rifle across his broad chest, waiting for something to happen.

The rancher knew the Wolf was confident he would not fire the first shot. Men like Adams had an unwritten code by which they lived. A set of rules carved into their very being. A code which creatures such as the Wolf were always willing to exploit.

'Adams.' The unmistakable voice of

the Wolf screamed out from across the distance between them.

Gene Adams felt a trickle of sweat running down from beneath his ten-gallon hat as it made its way towards his bandanna.

'I hear you, Wolf.'

'This is between you and me, Adams.' The Wolf's voice echoed round the fort again.

Adams remained close to the wooden upright as he stared out through the rain at the line of horsemen.

'Agreed.'

The Wolf jabbed his spurs deeply into his horse's flesh, making the animal take a few steps forward before dragging his reins up again.

'Tell your friends why they are gonna die, Adams. Tell them how they will die because they are backing you up.'

The rancher glared out at the devil rider. It took every ounce of his resolve not to shoot the creature out of his saddle. He knew the Wolf would not hesitate if their positions were reversed.

Gritting his teeth he managed to control his tone of voice as he returned the banter.

'I thought you were still locked up, Wolf.'

The rider raised his rifle and fired into the air angrily.

'Have you told them why they'll die, Adams?'

Gene Adams glanced across at his two young wranglers. Both men touched the brims of their Stetsons to the big man at almost the same time. Suddenly he felt as if a great burden had been lifted off his broad shoulders as he smiled.

'My men know exactly why they are gonna try real hard at killing you and your henchmen, Wolf,' Adams growled loudly across the sodden range between them.

'This is just between you and me, Adams,' the Wolf called out mockingly. 'Is the big rancher too afraid to come out and face his executioner?'

'Keep talking, Wolf,' Adams taunted.

'How does it feel to be imprisoned, Adams?'

Adams sighed heavily.

'You went to jail when you should have been lynched, Wolf.'

'Come out and face me. Face me like a man, Adams.' the Wolf demanded vainly.

'I don't think so,' the rancher muttered quietly under his breath.

For what felt like an eternity, only the eerie pounding of the perpetual rain made any noise out on the forlorn range. It was beginning to brighten up far away in the distance as clouds began to yield to the blazing sun. Yet above the silent fort the sky remained a swirling mass of angry rain-clouds content to continue spitting their misery down on the mournful scene of carnage.

Adams held a gloved hand up to his two men who were waiting for a signal to begin squeezing the triggers of the rifles tied to the hands of their dead companions. They could not get any wetter than they already were. Only their Stetsons did what they were designed to do and kept their heads dry at least. Watching and waiting now became their only thought. Patience was making them virtuous in the midst of adversity.

Adams watched the horses being spurred ruthlessly and forced closer yet again.

'When do we start shooting, Gene?' Larry called out as he glimpsed the danger edging slowly nearer.

'Easy, son.' Adams swallowed hard.

'I'm a tad edgy, Gene,' Happy shouted across from one tower to the next.

'You and me both, Happy,' Adams admitted.

Then suddenly the cantering outlaws lowered their long rifles within seconds of one another. The mechanisms were cocked almost in unison and the carbines exploded into action.

The talking had now ended. Now it was time for the Wolf to use his fire-power in order to bring Adams out of the fort gates with his arms raised. The crazed outlaw knew the rancher would never allow his men to be destroyed to save his own bacon. Men like Gene Lon Adams had a sense of right. To the outlaw, this was a weakness.

The Wolf would use this against him.

The air became filled with deadly venom as the riders blasted up at the figures beyond the wooden fort walls.

'Now,' screamed Adams to his two terrified cowboys over the sound of deafening rifle-fire.

15

'Hear that, old-timer?' Johnny Puma asked Tomahawk as he lay against the almost vertical rock-face.

Tomahawk used his hatchet to drag himself level with the young cowboy, then stopped to regain his wind.

'The shooting has started up all over again, Johnny.'

'At least that means the boys ain't dead.'

'It only means at least one of them is still alive.'

Johnny stared up in awe at the final thirty or so feet of their climb, then looked across at his partner.

'Do ya reckon we are gonna make it in time to help Gene and the boys, old-timer?'

Tomahawk opened his left eye and glared at his friend.

'We gotta make it to the top of this

mountain before we can help anyone, boy.'

The younger man scraped his boots against the wet stone until eventually he felt enough resistance to lever himself up another few inches to where he could just make out a small fingerhold. He gasped for air as he found himself listening to the gunfire beyond the high rim of the rock formation.

'You OK, Johnny?' Tomahawk asked, trying to keep his body as close to the rock-face as he could.

'I guess so.' Johnny dug his gloved fingers into a small crack a couple of feet above his head and dragged his soaked body upward until the pointed boot-toe of his right foot slipped into an inch-wide fault. Then he rested again, trying not to think of how far below them their horses waited. How quickly they would bridge that distance if they were to fall.

Tomahawk steadied himself before raising the Indian axe and smashing it into the smooth rock above him. He twisted the deadly weapon until he was confident the razor-sharp gleaming metal was in deep enough to hold his weight before hauling himself level with Johnny once again. The gunfire grew louder the further the determined pair managed to inch their way up the mountain of wet stone. Now it seemed to be echoing about them off other higher crags.

Both the men knew they were committed to this perilous route and there was no alternative now. Every inch they managed to move up seemed to take a lifetime to complete. The past ten feet of their climb had become more and more testing but they had to struggle on.

Glancing away from the rock-face, Tomahawk could see the sun breaking through the storm clouds in the distance. If it were only to stop raining, he knew they might have a fighting chance.

Silently the two men looked at one

another before continuing their treacherous ascent. As the rain stabbed mercilessly into their faces they gritted their teeth and headed up towards the sound of death above them.

Every sinew in their bodies cried out as they got closer and closer to their goal. Water streamed down towards the cowboys, making every movement a dice with death. Only raw courage and dogged determination kept the pair headed upward.

★   ★   ★

Moving speedily from one soldier's body to the next, Happy Summers and Larry Baker did as they had been instructed by Adams. Squeezing a trigger, cocking the rifle before moving to the next. Adams leaned against the upright within the tower as he fired down into the cocktail of rain and gunsmoke. Bullets from the Wolf and his men's Winchesters blasted at the top of the fort walls, sending a million splinters floating into the air. As Happy slid his index finger into yet another trigger guard he felt the trooper's dead body being hit by a volley of bullets. Then, he saw another of the bodies close to Larry being hit with so many well-aimed shots it fell backwards off the parapet and landed in the quagmire below.

Happy and Larry were not aiming the rifles placed under the armpits of the dead soldiers. They were just pulling the triggers as Adams had told them to do in order to draw their enemy's lethal fire.

Even the driving rain seemed incapable of keeping the acrid aroma of gunsmoke from filling the air.

Within five minutes the firing ceased and the three Bar 10 ranch men heard the sound of the outlaws riding away out of range, towards the rocky gulch.

Adams waited for the smoke to be washed away by the rain before he risked moving close to the wall to investigate.

He sighed heavily as he saw two of the outlaws' lifeless bodies beneath the walls of Fort Boone whilst the Wolf had led his remaining men several hundred yards away. There were still at least a dozen or more heavily armed outlaws milling around their evil leader. Too many, Adams thought. Too many.

Happy Summers looked across at Larry who in turn cast his attention over towards the rancher.

'Is it over, Gene?'

Adams grabbed a box of shells from the wooden decking and hurriedly began loading his rifle.

'Not hardly, Happy. Their rifles are out of shells and they've just moved out of range to reload.'

Larry quickly checked the bodies along the parapet. Most were torn to shreds by the continuous barrage of bullets. Two had been blasted off the wooden walkway completely and now rested in the mud below.

'Should we load these rifles again, Gene?'

Adams pushed the final round into the cartridge chamber of his rifle and cocked it before looking up.

'We ain't got enough time. Grab some of the rifles off the other bodies on the west wall and switch them for the empty ones, boys.'

Adams had hardly finished his sentence when his eyes narrowed and he saw the riders returning fast. Lifting one of the dead troopers off the floor, the rancher laid the stiff corpse in the corner of the tower and knelt behind it. Taking careful aim he waited as the horsemen thundered towards the fort. He glanced across at his two men as they tried frantically to get enough rifles from the other dead soldiers, and felt sweat rolling down his spine. Adams had known fear before; it was part of living in Texas and being a real Texan, part of what it meant to be out on the vast ranges where the law seldom visited. Fear was part and parcel of the West. Being afraid meant you were still alive. Yet as he watched the riders charging straight at the fort, he knew this was a different sort of fear.

Maybe it was the familiar shrilling scream which came from the demented throat of the Wolf. A sound which had chilled his bones before. Whatever the reason for his trepidation, Adams knew he would not be feeling half as anxious if Tomahawk and Johnny were at his side instead of the inexperienced Happy and Larry.

As his gloved finger gently teased the rifle trigger and he watched another of the Wolf's henchmen hit the mud, he began to wonder if they could resist so many ruthless killers for much longer.

Then Adams noticed that the rain had stopped falling. As the second phase of the battle raged and he felt the wall absorbing the bullets of men intent on killing him, he knew they were running out of time as well as ammunition.

The clouds parted above them and the fort became bathed in sunshine. Adams worked his rifle for all it was worth, trying to claim further victims. Choking gunsmoke filled the air making his targets disappear from view.

He checked over his shoulder to watch as Happy and Larry continued firing the rifles down at the shrieking riders. Then, moving towards the edge of the tower, Adams tried to pick out the Wolf amid the crazed outlaws in the rising smoke of heated carbine fire. A bullet came suddenly out of the air and took his black ten-gallon hat off his head, revealing his white hair. The rancher ducked and moved down on to the parapet towards his faithful wranglers. As he reached Larry's side he paused.

The young cowboy glanced at him and looked alarmed.

'You're bleeding, Gene.'

Adams touched his head and felt the graze. Looking at his gloved fingers he saw his own blood.

'Hold on for another few minutes and they'll have to head back to the rocks to reload, boys.'

Larry squeezed another of the numerous triggers as he edged back along the line of ghost troopers.

'We ain't got many rounds left, Gene.'

Adams rested as he felt the heat from the sun on his face for the first time in days. Then the firing ceased once more as the riders again rode away out of range in order to reload their weaponry.

The rancher knew the Wolf and his gang had taken every box of ammunition from the fort when they had killed the soldiers. All he and his two wranglers had was what they had brought to this place in the chuck-wagon. As he had not expected to be riding into a war, it was not enough.

Larry raised himself up and glanced out at the distant riders before turning to Adams, whose face was etched with a vivid red trail of blood as it seeped from the graze upon his head down to his neck.

'You sure you're OK, Gene?'

Adams ran a glove across the blood

and wiped it along his pants.

'Just a scratch, Larry.'

Happy scrambled up beside them.

'I reckon we ought to check how much ammunition we've got left, Gene.'

'Do it,' Adams said.

Larry Baker propped the bullet-ridden bodies back against the walls again.

'It don't seem right using these dead folks like this.'

'It ain't right, son. I'm proud of you for knowing that without anyone having to spell it out for you. Trouble is, we have to do this. These bodies are soaking up most of the Wolf's bullets.'

'I guess so.' Larry nodded as he placed the last corpse over the wooden wall.

Adams got to his feet and loaded his rifle once more. Looking at the empty box of shells in his hand he began to sweat.

'How many of them are still in the saddle?'

Larry screwed up his eyes as he tried to count the distant killers.

'Nine or more. Maybe ten, it's hard to figure.'

Adams rested his hands on the back of one of the dead soldiers and stared out at the Wolf and his cohorts.

'I count ten.'

'Ten ain't too many, is it?' Larry's voice suddenly sounded less positive.

'Nope. Ten ain't too many for Bar 10 cowboys, Larry,' Adams heard himself saying as he patted the cowboy on the back.

The young man seemed to find comfort in the words of his boss and he relaxed.

Then Adams shrugged thoughtfully as he studied the far-off gang of riders.

'They ain't coming back just yet, Larry. Look over yonder.'

Larry raised his hand to shield the sun from his tired eyes and gazed out into the distance.

'They're dismounting, Gene. Have they given up? Is it finally over?'

'The Wolf don't quit so easily, Larry,' Adams drawled.

'Then why ain't they coming in shooting again?'

Gene Adams narrowed his eyes and rested his chin on the back of his gloved hand as he thought about the question and the chilling array of options available to the Wolf.

16

The three Bar 10 cowboys had waited in vain for over four hours for the Wolf to do something. During that time the sun had risen higher in the sky until it seemed to be hovering directly over the fort, blazing its merciless venom down upon the weary occupants. Now there was no hint of the rain storm which had haunted the previous night and most of the morning. The wooden walls creaked as the sun drew every last ounce of moisture out of the decaying structure. Larry Baker rested in one tower facing the distant outlaws, clutching nervously at his Winchester whilst directly opposite in the north tower, the well-built Happy Summers also kept his eyes peeled for danger. From their high vantage points, nothing could approach Fort Boone from either the front or sides. This was a totally alien situation to the two wranglers. Surrounded by death and squaring up to experienced killers was a trail neither man had ever ridden before. This was not their fight, it never had been. Yet they were Gene Adams' Bar 10 men and that meant something to them. It meant you stayed loyal. You stood shoulder to shoulder with the tall white-haired rancher. You fought and perhaps you died.

At least the shingle-covered roof-tops of the towers kept the blazing sun off the two cowboys' necks. Yet with the rising temperature, the aroma of decaying fallen men filled the afternoon air once again.

The parade-ground was now baked as rock hard as it had been when Adams and his men first arrived within the relative safety of its high walls. Now it seemed to be getting hotter with every passing minute.

Gene Adams had come down from the walls and spent the last hour trying to comfort the horribly injured Tom Conners as he lay within the chuck-wagon. Only water sweetened with canned milk passed over the blue lips of the young cowboy now. Even swallowing this took every ounce of effort Tom could muster. His eyes were hollow as he sucked in air tentatively between sips.

'We'll get out of this mess real soon, Tom,' Gene Adams told the almost lifeless wrangler.

'You manage to get any of them?'

'We cut a few down.'

'Why are they doing this?'

Adams looked away as guilt filled his soul.

'They're after me, Tom.'

'Who?' Tom, blinked as if trying to focus.

'A critter known as the Wolf.' Adams found even the name tasted like poison in his mouth.

'The Wolf? I never heard of him.'

'It was a tad before you came to the Bar 10.'

'Why? Why would he wanna get you, Gene?'

167

'It don't matter none.' Adams swallowed and he began to wonder if he might be able to stop this insane carnage by simply stepping outside the gates of Fort Boone and squaring up to the Wolf. Would it end then, or would even his own death just leave the three cowboys to an even worse fate?

'I'm busted up real bad, Gene,' Tom said in a faint, feeble voice as the rancher cooled his brow with a damp cloth.

'You ain't too healthy, Tom,' Adams admitted as his thoughts drifted to his crazed foe outside the fortress. What was the evil creature planning? Had the Wolf stopped the frontal assault simply because he had lost three more of his men? Adams knew the Wolf could not care less about the vermin who rode in his shadow, so why had he stopped?

'I'm gonna die pretty soon, Gene.' The youngster sighed as he looked up at the older man.

Adams wiped the cloth over Tom's face once more, trying to think of the right words. Adams prided himself on his own honesty but this seemed a time when lies were justified.

'You only need a little rest, Tom.'

Tom Conners' face somehow smiled. He knew the big man well and could see the pain etched in the tanned features above him.

'Promise me something, Gene?' Tom's voice faltered as he spoke.

'Anything, Tom. What do you want, son?' Adams leaned on an elbow beside the once-expert horseman.

'Promise me when I die you'll bury me on the Bar 10 beneath the bluebonnets?'

Adams's eyes narrowed as he lowered his head.

'You ain't gonna . . . '

'Promise me, Gene.' Tom stared straight into Adams's face. Adams seemed visibly upset at the thought of losing one of the best men who had ever saddled up and ridden a horse with the Bar 10 brand.

'I promise I'll take you back home,

Tom.' Adams thought about the lush pastures to the east of the vast Bar 10 ranch. Pastures covered in a blanket of bluebonnet flowers as far as the eye could see. There was no sweeter fragrance, nothing so utterly different from the aroma of death which filled their nostrils within this unholy place.

'Thanks, Gene,' Tom said, shutting his eyes for the last time.

Closing the lifeless lids of the cowboy now riding a more peaceful trail, Adams gritted his teeth before climbing out of the chuck-wagon. It took a few seconds for him to wipe the last of the tears from his eyes with his gloved hands and compose himself. Seconds which reinforced his resolve.

The Wolf was not going to win this battle.

17

Gazing hypnotically through the shimmering heat haze across at the distant fort, whilst his henchmen consumed bottle after bottle of salvaged army whiskey, the Wolf smiled. To him, it was all now going to plan. The rain which had delayed his putting the final chapter of his maniacal scheme together had ended. Now he would literally light the fuse.

The Wolf and his men had been here for nearly four days since riding from Painted Rock after sending the bogus wire to Gene Adams. That had been the beginning. Hidden amongst the rocks they had waited for the garrison's weekly patrol to ride away from Fort Boone, leaving it vulnerable.

After the Wolf had helped his bloodthirsty gang in killing every living creature in and around the fort, he then planted his trump card beneath its wooden walls. Twenty sticks of dynamite in two ten-stick bundles were linked together by a pair of two-hundred-yard-long fuse-wires, buried a few inches below the surface of the flat range.

Now as the crazed killer looked at the ends of the two fuse wires poking out of the ground next to his string of horses he could not help from laughing out loud. The Wolf had known their effectiveness would be less deadly during the savage rainstorm. Now the sun had dried out his target and any explosion would be as devastating as he had imagined during his five years of incarceration.

But he would not light the fuse just yet.

Adams had not suffered nearly enough. The rancher had to suffer as he had done for a half-decade. Adams had to be broken not just physically but mentally first. Then and only then would he push the smouldering tip of a cigar on to the ends of those waiting fuses.

Exhaling smoke from his broken lips, the Wolf studied the blue sky overhead. Now there were no more clouds. It would not rain again before he executed the grand finale of his vengeful plan and stole the last remnants of Adams's hope and then his sanity until it echoed his own twisted mind.

★   ★   ★

The heavens had ceased their cruel punishment long enough for the two bedraggled Bar 10 cowboys to complete their death-defying feat. Johnny Puma and Tomahawk had lain exhausted for an hour after reaching the top of their valiant climb. The sun had dried them out long before they had begun their trek down through the winding maze of towering rocks in search of the bushwhackers. Since the gunfire had ceased there was no indication as to which direction they ought to be heading.

With his ancestral survival instincts honed to the very pitch of perfection over countless decades, Tomahawk led the way down through the blazing sun-bleached rocks. Johnny walked in his partner's tracks. Every step they took brought them closer to a place neither of them truly wanted to reach. Pausing only for sips from their solitary canteen, the pair knew they might just have left their intervention too late.

Neither man mentioned their fellow Bar 10 comrades during the blistering journey. The younger man toyed with his matched pair of Colt .45s, his eyes scanning around them as they travelled down the dusty route between the innumerable rocks. He was ready to draw on the first man to show his face or wave a weapon in their direction, and to kill if necessary. Johnny Puma had been known by a very different name when he was a youth. He had used his guns with such expertise, they had become part of his very being. Only

Gene Adams had managed to tame the young man before fate could step in and destroy his soul. Adams had given him the name of Johnny Puma and saved him from himself just in time.

Now Johnny wondered if he had lost the man he respected so much to those deafening bullets which he had heard ringing out whilst they had been climbing the rock-face. Without Adams, could there be a Johnny Puma? Could there even be a Bar 10 ranch?

Tomahawk knew as he led the way down the unyielding trail that the kid was becoming angry. Angry because they might arrive at Fort Boone to discover nothing but bodies.

Gripping the handle of his Indian hatchet in his weathered hand, Tomahawk too was ready for anyone who might leap out and attempt to dry-gulch them. His bones had never ached as much as they did at this moment. Sleep seemed to be a distant memory now as he followed his nose along the twisting route, ever downward into a place silent and eerily unfamiliar.

Then, as they rounded a large rock higher than a two-storey saloon, Tomahawk stopped and lowered himself on to one knee.

Johnny edged up and lay quietly down alongside him.

'What do you see?' Johnny whispered over Tomahawk's shoulder.

'Buzzards up high and vermin downwind.'

The young cowboy had already drawn one of his pistols as he squinted out into the bright vista before them. For a moment he did not quite comprehend the words but soon gathered their true meaning.

Circling high in the distance, half a dozen vultures floated above the fort on the warm thermals. Johnny knew they could scent a carcass a dozen miles away. Then his eyes followed Tomahawk's axe as it pointed down into the hollow, two hundred feet below them. A string of horses behind an equal number of men. Men who seemed content to drink the entire contents of the liquor boxes stacked beside their camp-fire.

'Who are they, Tomahawk?'

'I reckon they must be the rats who have been doing all the shooting, Johnny.' The old man raised a hand to shadow his eyes as he vainly tried to see if there were any recognizable faces amongst the bunch.

'Why are they holed up down there?' Johnny posed yet another question which had no obvious answer.

Tomahawk turned and rested his old spine against the smooth rock as he tried to figure it out.

'Our boys must still be OK, Johnny.'

'How do you figure that?'

'Stands to reason. If they were all dead, those critters up in the sky yonder would be down there picking their bones clean.' Tomahawk raised a bushy eyebrow and looked straight at his friend.

Johnny nodded in agreement.

'Gene might still be alive?'

'Reckon there's a real good chance he is.'

The younger man rubbed his mouth and breathed heavily at the thought they might still be able to assist their trapped comrades, who might still be alive and waiting for anyone to help them. Johnny wanted to rush down towards the outlaws with both guns blazing, but the words of Gene Adams kept returning to haunt him. He had always been a hothead and it had cost him dearly in the past. Now he had to think first, just the way the wiser rancher would wish. For the first time since he and Tomahawk had set out on this trail he felt the knots in his stomach beginning to relax.

'What we gonna do?'

'First we rest up a while and try and work out a plan, boy.'

Johnny raised his gun.

'I could go down there and kill most of them before they knew what was happening, Tomahawk.'

The older man shook his head slowly

as he unscrewed the stopper on the canteen.

'Nope. That'll only get you deader than whatever it is them buzzards are smelling, Johnny.'

Johnny's eyes narrowed.

'Then what?'

'I'm thinking, boy. I'm thinking real hard,' Tomahawk said, before putting the canteen to his lips and taking a mouthful of the warm water.

'Do it faster, my trigger finger's itchy.' Johnny leaned back next to his pal and reluctantly rested.

18

Gene Adams led his saddled chestnut mare solemnly across the parade ground towards the secured fort gates. Bewildered by the sight, the two wranglers came hurriedly down their ladders and ran up to the grim-faced rancher.

'What ya doing, Gene?' Larry asked as he reached the man, who continued leading his horse straight at the gates.

'You figuring on heading out?' Happy panted as he too reached the steady-paced rancher.

Adams did not pause but kept walking, his eyes trained on the massive gates ahead of him.

'Gene?' Larry grabbed at the sleeve of the big man until Adams finally halted and stared at the ground before him.

'What you doing?' Happy asked as he

moved in front of his boss and held out a hand.

Adams raised his head and looked at each of their faces in turn. He had not told either of them about Tom. There had not been the words within him capable of telling them their friend was dead. They were scared enough.

'I'm the one he wants, boys.'

'You figuring on going out there to face the Wolf?' Larry raised his arms into the air. 'I ain't gotta lot of smarts but even I know when a varmint is ready to kill me. The Wolf will just split you up the middle and feed you to them damn buzzards, Gene.'

'You gonna leave us to try and fight alone, Gene?' Happy moved about the two men kicking at the parade ground dust. 'Me and Larry can't shoot better than a pair of spinsters. You know that. If you head out and get yourself killed we ain't got no chance at all.'

Adams heaved his huge chest as the madness suddenly left him.

'I intended killing him first, boys.'

'I intended to marry me a rich widow woman before I was twenty but you don't always get what you want in this damn world, Gene.' Happy shrugged.

Adams nodded.

'It might be our only chance. I used to be a pretty good shot with these guns.'

The two younger men stood their ground before the big man defiantly. They were not going to let him pass, and he knew it. Adams stared at them as they squared up to him and finally released the grip on his reins. In all his days, he had never been in such a fix as this. The Wolf had them exactly where he wanted them, Adams thought. Trapped like rats. Revenge had turned a mere maniac into something far worse.

Walking slowly to the ladder leading up to the northern tower, the rancher hesitated and glanced over his broad shoulder at the two cowboys.

'Thanks, boys,' he said, quietly acknowledging his own lapse.

'The Bar 10 don't need two Johnny

Pumas, Gene.' Happy nodded as he picked up the reins of the chestnut mare and began leading it back to the other horses beyond the wagon.

Adams forced a smile as he climbed back up the ladder to the high platform of the tower with Larry on his heels, Staring out at the view he suddenly noticed a lone rider heading towards them, holding a white flag tied to the barrel of a carbine.

'Who in tarnation is that?' Larry gasped.

'The Wolf!' Adams exclaimed.

Larry grabbed at a rifle resting against the wall.

'And the bastard's in range. Even I can't miss from this distance.'

Adams forced his friend's rifle down as he edged closer to the tower wall.

'You can't shoot a man carrying a white flag, boy.'

'Why not? He ain't shown no mercy to these troopers or Tom or the animals, Gene.' Larry snarled.

For a brief moment Gene Adams felt

himself agreeing with his friend but then he remembered his code of honour. No matter how much he knew the Wolf deserved to be blasted off his saddle, he could not be party to such a cowardly act.

'We ain't sinking to his level, Larry. That ain't the Bar 10 way. Never has been, never will be,' Adams announced.

'But if we kill him, it's all over,' Larry muttered.

'You gotta admit, he's got tar, Larry,' Adams said angrily watching the rider.

For a few minutes the two cowboys waited silently in the tower as the solitary horseman drew ever closer. Never had any rider been observed so intently as they watched the Wolf. Holding reins in one hand and the Winchester bearing the white flag of truce in the other he aimed his horse straight at the tower.

As he drew up below the tower, the Wolf looked up defiantly into the eyes of the rancher he despised so deeply. Their mutual hatred seemed to bridge the gap between them. It was as if Larry Baker had become invisible as the two men's eyes burned into one another. The Wolf no longer looked as he had when their paths had first crossed. Now he glared up from beneath hair that was matted and long. A beard covered the better part of his face and chest but the eyes were unchanged.

Evil eyes which betrayed the sickness festering within his rancid soul.

Adams had never known himself to feel as he did now, looking down at this cruel, evil man. It frightened the rancher to know that he too had such ugliness lurking within himself.

'Gene Adams.' The Wolf's voice seemed almost to choke upon the name as it passed his lips.

Adams nodded.

'Wolf.'

'You ready to come out and face me like a man?'

The question hung in the air, taunting the rancher.

'First I wanna know why you did all this,' Adams replied, waving his arm around the scene. 'How come you had to kill so many folks and critters? If you wanted me, why didn't you just come looking for me?'

'Could any man get past all your cowboys, Adams?'

Adams considered the question.

'Would a real man kill so many just for revenge?'

The Wolf shook his head before answering:

'When you spend five years planning something it just kinda grows and grows inside you, Adams.'

'Like a cancer.'

The Wolf nodded and looked discreetly at the foot of the fortress gates for signs that his hidden explosives were still where he had buried them. The ground was untouched. They were still there undisturbed.

'Do you like being caged like an animal, Adams?'

'Nope. Can't say I like it, Wolf.'

'For five years I rotted away in that prison until my men bust me loose, Adams,' the Wolf snarled. 'I've only had you pinned in here for less than a day and you don't cotton to it.'

'But why kill so many when you just wanted me?'

'I had to kill them, Adams. It was in my plan.' The Wolf wrapped his reins around his saddle horn, then drew a cigar from his shirt-pocket and bit off its end. He placed it into his mouth.

Adams watched as he ignited a match with his thumbnail and sucked the flame into the long brown weed. A plume of thick grey smoke rose from the cigar as the smoker glanced down once more at the foot of the gate-posts. Suddenly Gene Adams became aware of his enemy's interest in the seemingly ordinary piece of ground. He rubbed his chin thoughtfully.

'You willing to let my men go if I square up to you, Wolf?'

There was no immediate reply. The outlaw sucked on the cigar and savoured the taste of the smoke as it drifted out of his mouth and hung in the hot still air.

'I'm willing but my men might just think a mite differently, Adams.'

Adams growled down at the man.

'Those spineless vermin will do as you order, Wolf. They ain't got the brains to act on their own, and you know it.'

The Wolf glanced up at the angry rancher.

'True. Very true. The problem is they've tasted blood, Adams, and when a critter tastes blood he kinda gets a hankering for it.'

Adams swallowed hard as he heard Happy and Larry coming up the ladder behind him. Waving a gloved hand at the cowboys to remain out of sight, Adams continued talking to the outlaw.

'So you ain't gonna give me your word?'

'Would my word be worth a plug nickel to you, Adams?' The Wolf blew out a long line of smoke as he considered his plan and how sweetly it was taking shape unknown to the men above him.

'Maybe not, but you owe me something for not shooting you as you rode up, Wolf,' insisted the rancher grimly.

The Wolf held the cigar between his teeth and unwrapped his reins with his free hand. Somewhere within the depths of his crazed brain, a dark messenger was telling him to take the next step.

'I knew you would never shoot a man carrying a flag of truce, Adams. It's a mistake which has and will continue to cost you dearly.'

Suddenly, away in the distance at the Wolf's encampment the sound of gunfire echoed across the wide range. The outlaw glanced through the heat haze in the direction of the commotion before returning his attention to Adams.

'What's happening, Wolf?' Adams yelled down at the rider.

'Seems like my boys have had a little too much whiskey.' The Wolf grinned through the smoke of his cigar.

Adams stared into the shimmering haze vainly trying to see the distant gun battle which echoed over Fort Boone like thunder.

Before the Bar 10 man could speak again, he saw the Wolf turning his horse's head away from the fort whilst lowering the rifle's barrel and firing up at them defiantly.

Larry screamed as he fell backwards clutching his shoulder.

As the cowboy landed at Happy Summer's feet, blood spurted out from the neat wound over the decking.

Gene Adams looked down in horror at his fallen pal and then back over the wooden wall at the Wolf galloping away. Drawing his gold plated pistols from their holsters, Adams aimed and fired twice with both weapons in quick succession. The Wolf's horse fell heavily, bringing the retreating outlaw down with it in a cloud of dust.

Returning the guns speedily back to his holsters, Adams climbed over the tower wall and paused for a split second.

'Cover me if his men try to help him, Happy,' Adams called out as he dropped down to the ground outside the fort. Turning in the direction of the fallen horse as a cloud of dust hung over the impact, he started to run.

Tossing his hat to one side, Adams ran furiously at the Wolf as he staggered to his feet.

Before the outlaw knew what was happening, the tall rancher had thrown his full weight into the thin emaciated centre of him, sending them both cartwheeling to the ground. A gun somehow appeared in the hand of the Wolf and a bullet blasted between the two wrestling men. The smell of gunsmoke and burning clothing filled the air as they rolled over the ground. Adams clutched at the wrist of his adversary, using his superior weight and strength to keep the pistol away from himself. A blinding flash and another deafening shot blasted from the gun as the Wolf squeezed the trigger again.

Adams smashed his fist into the jaw of the bearded man and fell over with him yet again. Once more the gun exploded as they hit the dust. The heat burnt into them as they struggled feverishly across the dry ground.

Trying to keep the agile outlaw down was a lot harder than Adams had anticipated. Five years of breaking stones in a prison quarry had given the crazed killer muscles where once there had been nothing but soft flesh.

A bony fist caught Adams just above his left eye splitting the skin and sending blood rushing down his face. Yet before the next blow could find its mark, Adams forced the gun clutched in the Wolf's hand down across his skull.

The outlaw went limp as Adams struck him twice more on his bearded chin. Somehow the rancher managed to get back up on to his feet. He stared down at the pitiful outlaw lying flat on his back. Adams touched his eye and looked at the blood on his glove. He turned to stare out across the range, towards the sound of gunfire.

Then be remembered the Wolf's interest in the ground outside the fort gates and began walking unsteadily back to them. Before he reached them, they opened and Happy Summers appeared, clutching his pistol anxiously.

'Is he done for, Gene?' the wrangler asked, keeping his gun trained on the fallen outlaw.

'He's out cold,' Adams replied as he reached the base of one of the tall gate posts and kneeling.

'He ain't dead?' Happy snarled.

'How's Larry?' Adams asked as his gloved hands dug at the ground.

Happy moved over the rancher.

'He's OK. The bullet went straight through him.'

Adams nodded and then paused as his fingers found the fuse wire and then the sticks of dynamite. Pulling the sticks carefully out of the ground, he tore the fuses out and laid the now harmless bundle on to the ground before rising.

'Dynamite?' Happy's voice dried up as he saw the ten sticks of explosives.

'The Wolf was busy before we showed up, Happy,' Adams said striding across to the opposite gate pole and repeating his actions.

The chubby wrangler was sweating far more than usual as he watched Adams making the second package of carefully bound dynamite sticks harmless.

'Is that it, Gene? There ain't no more, is there?'

Adams rested his spine against the high wall of the fort and closed his eyes for a moment as he tried to shake off the pain in his head. Blood dripped onto his shirt as he opened his eyes once more to look at his friend. Then he saw the Wolf moving over Happy's shoulder and dragged the cowboy away as he reached for his guns.

The blast that came from the

Winchester held in the hands of the crazed outlaw hit Adams in his ribs. The rancher was forced hard back into the wall. As he bounced off the wooden posts he fired both his gold-plated Colts in unison. Adams watched as the Wolf twisted into the air and fell like a discarded rag doll next to the body of his horse.

As the gunsmoke cleared from his gun barrels, Gene Adams staggered into the arms of the terrified Happy Summers.

'You OK, Gene? Gene? Answer me, Gene.'

Adams raised his right hand and pointed his Colts into the distance.

'It ain't over, Happy,' Adams said as he felt the pain of the wound to his side ripping through him.

Happy turned and looked to see where his boss was aiming his golden Colts. Dust was rising from the hoofs of riders heading towards them.

'When's it gonna end?'

He dragged Adams inside the gates

and quickly checked his blood-soaked side.

'You're only winged, Gene.'

Adams looked out at the dust of the riders, then grabbing his ranny's shoulder he laughed out loud.

'I reckon its over right now, Happy. Look.'

Happy raised a hand to shield his eyes from the sun and squinted out at the approaching riders. Suddenly he realized he was looking at Johnny Puma and Tomahawk thundering towards them.

'I don't get it, Gene.'

'Neither do I, but who gives a damn?' Adams sighed happily.

★　★　★

Major Bellamy and his patrol had arrived back at Fort Boone less than two hours after the battle had ended. Greeted by the surviving Bar 10 rancher and his men, he was told the full ugly story by the injured Gene

Adams. Apparently Tomahawk and Johnny had waited for the Wolf to leave his men drinking their fill of the garrison's liquor supply before striking. Although they had not gone into any detail, it was clear that they had not allowed a single member of the gang to survive. The wounds on their bodies showed clearly that they had been in a fight to match or even better the one Gene Adams had waged with the Wolf.

The men of the Bar 10 hit the trail for home the following day, after helping the soldiers bury their dead comrades. It was a sad line of horsemen who surrounded the chuck-wagon and its precious cargo. A cargo Gene Adams had promised to return to the pastures of his ranch.

Finale

Every cowboy who rode for the Bar 10 ranch stood solemnly around the simple grave of Tom Conners. Gene Adams held his Bible in his gloved left hand after saying a few well-chosen words and nodded as his men made their way quietly back to their horses.

It was a beautiful pasture covered with bluebonnet flowers from one horizon to the other. This was a special place on the Bar 10. Here no longhorn steers grazed as they did across the rest of the vast Texan ranch.

Here it was peaceful and quiet. Only the songs of the birds disturbed the natural splendour.

Tomahawk stepped close to Gene Adams, who was still nursing his wounds. Johnny Puma walked away with his arm around Happy Summers' shoulder, while Larry waited in a buckboard amid the other cowboys.

'Tom was a good kid, Gene.'

'Yep. A good kid like all our boys.' Adams sighed as he slipped the book inside his deep jacket-pocket.

'How come we brought him back here to bury, Gene?' The old man gripped his hat as he stared at the grave.

Adams rested a hand upon the thin shoulder of his oldest pal and sighed.

'I made him a promise, Tomahawk.'

Tomahawk shook his head as he thought about their ordeal.

'All that killing because of a crazy man. It just don't figure.'

Adams turned and began walking back across the pasture of wild flowers toward their waiting horses with the old-timer at his side.

'It's nice here,' he commented.

Tomahawk paused and looked back at the grave bathed in gentle sunlight filtered by the tall trees.

'Tom chose a good place to rest, Gene.'

'I can't think of a better one to spend eternity.'

'Me neither.'

Adams stepped into his stirrup and mounted the chestnut mare as his old friend climbed on to the buckboard next to the quiet Larry Baker. Turning his tall horse the rancher began leading the riders down towards the heart of the Bar 10.

He had kept his promise to a dying wrangler.

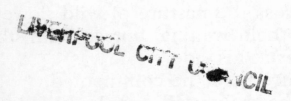